Unity and the Children

Richard L. Baldwin

To Marge,
thanks for all you
do for others!
Rich Baldwin

BUTTONWOOD PRESS
Haslett, Michigan

This book is a product of the imagination of the author. All the characters portrayed are fictitious. None of the events described occurred. The story has no purpose other than to entertain the reader.

Published by Buttonwood Press
PO Box 716
Haslett, Michigan 48840

Publisher's Cataloging-in-Publication Data
(Provided by Quality Books, Inc.)

Baldwin, Richard L.
    Unity and the children / by Richard L. Baldwin.
  -- 1st ed.
    p. cm.
    SUMMARY: A special visitor named Unity brings attitude changes to the Timber Ridge School, which serves children and young adults with severe to profound disabilities.
    ISBN: 0-9660685-3-X
    1. Special education--Juvenile fiction.
    2. Handicapped students--Juvenile fiction.
    3. Schools--Juvenile fiction.   I. Title.

    PZ7.B1895Uni 2000   [Fic]
                  QB199-1447

Printed by Sheridan Books
Printed in the United States of America

Dedication

This book is dedicated to people everywhere who have love within them—a love that can change hearts so as to unify souls in every environment.

Appreciation

Sincere appreciation is extended to the many people who have helped me arrive at an understanding that the spirit or soul within guides us to unity on a physical level.

Thank you Patty Baldwin for your love, support, and your belief in me.

Thank you Ed Birch for suggesting I apply my love of writing to my spiritual beliefs and understandings.

Thank you Bryn Fortune for listening, pushing and encouraging the creation of this book.

Thank you Kathy VanTol for giving me confidence.

Thank you Joyce Gard for your original painting of Unity.

Thank you Staci Galarowicz-Villarruel and Penny Zago for reading a draft and offering constructive comments.

Thank you Marilyn "Sam" Nesbitt for designing the cover, typesetting the manuscript, and preparing marketing materials.

Thank you Sheridan Books, especially Kathy King and Jean Schroeder, for guiding this book through production.

This book could not have been created without support from people skilled in wordsmithing. I am indebted to; Holly Sasso, my editor; and, to Joyce Wagner, my proofreader.

Then Yahweh answered and said. "Write the vision down. inscribe it on tablets to be easily read. since the vision is for its own time only: eager for its own fulfillment: it does not deceive: if it comes slowly. wait. for come it will. without fail."

Hab. 2:2-4

Foreword by Ed Birch

Through the voices of children and the guidance of "Unity," Rich takes us on a journey that challenges the practice of "separation" in our system of education. We are led to appreciate the need for "laws and regulations" when the rights of children with special needs were first recognized and provided by the public schools. We are equally led to understand the need to replace the reliance on "laws and regulations" in favor of "unity and love."

Rich's extensive experience as a teacher and administrator and his learning through a personal quest for spiritual understanding are brought together in *Unity and the Children*. From his professional experiences, he teaches us about the special education system, a system much too separate and segregated. Through his spiritual understandings he teaches us that we are all "connected" by a spiritual love, a love manifested in "unity" and "inclusion" rather than separateness.

In *Unity and the Children*, the subject is education and the special needs of children. But the message is equally relevant for those who see differences in people because of the color of their skin, the origin of their birth, or of their economic circumstances.

Consequently, his book is not just for educators and parents of students with special needs, but for anyone who is willing to be challenged on how they think about, and act toward, their brothers and sisters.

Ed Birch, Kalamazoo, Michigan

Foreword by L. Bryn Fortune

Over the past six years, I've had the pleasure of getting to know Rich. We were given this opportunity because he had developed a significant connection to my youngest daughter. Lindsay is a beautiful fourteen-year-old woman, who has with much grace, found her way through life facing all the challenges of being a person with "differing abilities" in the Western World. Living as a "full" member of our community, her path is framed with struggles. (No small accomplishment in the current configuration of our systemized culture!)

As a result of their connection, I have been blessed with the opportunity to both appreciate and learn from Rich's gift as a storyteller. We've exchanged conversation about our individual spiritual beliefs. Because of that connection, I was honored when five years ago Rich asked if I would read an early draft of the story that has become this book.

Part of the history of my growing spirituality involved a long sabbatical in the desert. As a seeker in the hot sand, I was surprised to discover my inability to find literature that gently and lovingly supported my journey. What struck me when I first read his story was the degree to which it could fill this void. So, with that as my backdrop, I began encouraging, (and yes, I suppose pushing) Rich to publish this sacred body of work. I believe this is one of his gifts that we all need him to share as a healer in our time. In order for us to collectively relearn how to be a loving and caring people, all of us must be given the chance to learn from our modern prophets.

So, for you as the reader, there is some reason your journey has led you to this book. I will close by saying, "Seek and you shall find. Knock and the door shall be opened." Seeking... stretching... growing... learning... opening. The true answer resides in every one of us.

L. Bryn Fortune, Farmington Hills, Michigan

Author's Introduction

As a high school student, I was active in the First Presbyterian Church of Grand Haven, Michigan. After an associate pastor had left to assume a pastoral position in another community, our minister, Reverend Wallace Robertson, asked me if I would read the Scripture and give the group prayer each Sunday for several months. I have a vivid memory of practicing the Bible reading and creating a prayer each week under his tutoring wing. After the service I would greet worshipers at the side door. Dr. Robertson invited me to attend the weekly staff meeting in the church. As an 18-year-old young man, I was feeling very comfortable experiencing a baptism of sorts for a future vocation.

While attending Alma College, for reasons I cannot recall, my interest shifted from the ministry to education. Having come up through the public schools in Grand Haven with a moderate hearing loss, I found my attention shifting to a relatively new direction, special education.

So, I transferred to Western Michigan University and majored in deaf education and eventually became a teacher of hearing impaired children at Kalamazoo Central High School and Milwood

Junior High School. I worked with Anne Genetti and Bernice Holland who, through their commitment and talent, taught me much about educating children. I then became a teacher of children with hearing impairments in Berrien Springs under the leadership of a committed and tireless educator, Andy Gantenbien. It was during this time that I found myself interested in pursuing my education in order to become a better teacher. I enrolled in Kansas University and three years later graduated with my Ed.D. Degree.

I taught at Kent State University (1973-75) and at Texas Tech University (1975-77). In 1977 I accepted a consultant position with the Michigan Department of Education. The federal government had recently mandated special education in 1975 (P.L. 94-142) and produced accompanying rules in 1977. Michigan's mandatory law had been in effect since 1971 (P.A. 198) and rules since 1973. The Michigan rules and the federal rules were often conflicting in terminology and in process. It was my job to coordinate these two sets of rules into one set of standards.

While at the Department of Education, I was enmeshed in all of the legal aspects of special education. I was responsible for monitoring the rules. It was my staff who went into school districts to see that schools were operating in compliance with the law, teachers were credentialed, and funds were appropriately managed.

Because of my responsibility to hold people accountable to the law, I would often be a barrier to those who wanted to try creative and innovative programs and services. I came to realize that while compliance with the law was valuable to parents and people in government, there didn't seem to be any correlation between quality programming and compliance with law and rule.

In 1990, I became Director of the Office of Special Education and found myself responsible for the entire system at the state level. I was immersed in law, rules, forms, policy, guidelines, and procedures. Almost everything that I dealt with was linked to law and rule.

Against this backdrop, I found within myself a need to tie my earlier spiritual career aspirations to my current career reality. I soon discovered a significant clash. The great spiritual thinkers were emphasizing a connectedness of souls and the importance of love as an alternative to laws controlling people that had evolved over centuries and still, I might add, exist today. The two systems were obviously bipolar. I came to the conflicted conclusion that I had become thoroughly entrenched in the legalistic and controlling aspects of state government, as my belief system continued to reside in the connectedness and love of my spiritual knowledge.

I watched, resisted, supported, and played through attempts of adults, government, and nationally known writers/speakers to change people's thinking about this separate system called "special education." The more I thought about it, I couldn't see any significant change coming because efforts at changing the system were being suggested to adults who had grown up with a separatist mindset. Teachers had learned in college that these children with labels were not their responsibility, but may belong to another set of teachers and specialists with special training, special forms, special classes, and special money. Administrators had special schools and agencies with people prepared to reinforce the separation between general and special education. Law wasn't changing hearts, and people who believed in separation weren't going to change the system.

One day my friend and mentor, Dr. Ed Birch, asked about my writing. Ed knew of my interest in spirituality and my years of experience in special education. He suggested that I write a story relating to children with disabilities. I went home that day and began to write *Unity and the Children*.

What became clear to me in telling this story is that the change would come from the children—not from law, not from politicians, not from government employees, nor from adults who had grown up in a separatist system. Ultimately the message that we will all open ourselves to, will come from the innocence of children. We are all connected through love. This is the same message passed from spiritual masters throughout time.

This book is fiction. It would please me beyond comprehension if someday, many years from now, a writer and/or publisher stumbled upon this story and based upon what was happening at the time, changed the genre from fiction to nonfiction.

Thank you for taking the time to read this introduction. Hopefully you now have a better understanding of the soul telling this story.

Chapter One

Students, teachers, and school aides had just finished recess and returned to the Timber Ridge School. Timber Ridge is a special school for young people with severe to profound disabilities who live in the Potawatomee Consolidated School District. The school was built in 1965 and was designed especially for children and young adults with the labels of retardation; trainably mentally handicapped, severely mentally handicapped, and severely multiply disabled. The classrooms were similarly labeled and so were the teachers.

A teacher aide came into the office and said to Harriet, the school secretary, "There's a lady out in the hall. She's been looking in the display cases and in the gym for several minutes."

"Thanks, Jane. I'll go find out who she is."

Harriet approached the woman who was standing outside the door to the gymnasium. She was watching students in wheelchairs trying to negotiate an obstacle course. They were preparing for Special Olympics competition at the Summer Games only a few months away.

"Hello," Harriet said with a smile.

"Oh, hello," Unity replied.

"Can I help you? Are you here to see someone?"

"I saw this school and decided to come in and see the young people," Unity remarked with a sense of calm and peace about her. She was clothed in a simple dress with a light coat to protect her from the slight chill in the spring air.

"Well, welcome to our school."

"Thank you."

"My name is Harriet Leiter, and you are?" Harriet asked, leading the stranger to identify herself.

"My name is Unity."

"That's a unique and beautiful name. I don't believe I've ever heard that name before."

Unity continued to watch the youth in the gym. Harriet was not sure what was going on. She thought that she might need to call security or maybe the police. It could be that this woman had walked away from a group home. *Maybe she has Alzheimer's and doesn't know where she is,* Harriet thought. But, Unity didn't seem like she would cause any trouble. In fact, being in her presence gave Harriet a calm feeling, a warm feeling that she couldn't describe.

"How can we help you at Timber Ridge School?" Harriet asked.

"I'd like to walk through this school," Unity responded.

"Are you related to one of the students?"

"Not directly. I'm related to everyone, as are you, but I'm not related in the sense you are asking."

"Are you a student at a college or university?"

"I'm a student of life, but I'm not a student in a school."

Unity and the Children

"Are you here representing any school, organization, or service agency?"

"I'm representing a consciousness that transcends schools, organizations, and service agencies; but I'm not representing any that you mentioned," Unity answered with a quiet assurance. She was not being difficult or answering in a sarcastic or condescending manner.

"I'm sorry, I don't understand. Why are you here and what can we do to help you?" Harriet asked, quite certain that this woman was probably harmless, but someone with a mental problem who had wandered into the school.

"I'm here because this is where I must be to do what must be done."

Harriet didn't understand Unity's answer and felt that it was time for the principal to get involved. "If you don't mind, I'd like you to meet the school principal. Would you please follow me to his office?" Harriet said as she turned toward the office and glanced back to see if Unity was following. When they arrived, Harriet said, "Please have a seat. I'll tell our principal, Mr. Brewer, that you're here."

Harriet went into Mr. Brewer's office and told him of Unity's presence. She told him of Unity's strange answers and that she didn't seem to be a threat to anyone. "In fact, there was a certain peace about her."

Mr. Brewer instructed Harriet to ask the woman to come into his office.

"Hello. I'm Philip Brewer, the principal of Timber Ridge School."

"My name is Unity. Thank you for making me feel welcome."

"Sure. How can we make your visit what you hope it to be?" Philip asked

Just before Unity spoke, one of the students came into Mr. Brewer's office. Harriet had stepped out to attend to an errand.

The student looked at Unity and slowly and painfully walked up to her and gave her a hug. It was a touching scene.

"Do you know Randy?" Mr. Brewer asked. "He's been a student here at Timber Ridge for almost fourteen years. He's seventeen years old now. He has cerebral palsy. He has difficulty walking and his speech is practically unintelligible. In this day and age of technology, he has made great gains using his computer to communicate with us. Most think that Randy is quite bright and understands what is being said, but until learning to use his computer, he has had little means of communicating his thoughts."

"Randy is special to me," Unity said.

Randy stood there and looked at Unity. He seemed to be in a daze and Philip wondered if the school nurse, Mrs. Sue Hickok, had misjudged his medication. Philip made a mental note to talk to the nurse when he finished with his guest.

Unity said, "It is good to see you Randy. Go back to your teacher and I'll see you again soon." With that, Randy did as Unity asked and left.

"Fine young man," Philip said with a smile and a sense of pride.

"Yes, he is."

"Well, as I was saying, how can we make your visit what you hoped it would be?"

"I would like to be free to walk throughout your school. I will not interrupt anyone. I will not talk to anyone unless they talk with me. I only want to watch people. Would that be all right with you?"

"Well, sure. That's fine. But, why are you here?" Philip inquired. "Nobody has ever come here just wanting to walk around."

Unity thought for a moment and lowered her head as if in prayer. She looked up after several seconds and said, "You cannot understand my visit now. I only ask that you be open to my presence and allow me to watch, talk with the people here, and become a visitor in your activities. I ask you to trust my presence. I assure you that I am no threat to you, your school or your policies. In time, it will all be purposeful and clear."

Philip thought it best, under the circumstances, to allow the woman to walk through the school. He would have to think about his instinct to notify the superintendent of the school district and perhaps the authorities. This was a strange encounter to say the least. For today, a walk through the school seemed harmless and the visitor did not seem to be a threat to anyone. After this quick assessment of the situation, he responded, "You are most welcome here, Unity. Feel free to walk through the school. If you wish to stop back and ask any questions, I will be here to answer them for you. Will we see you again?"

"Thank you. Yes, I will be with you again."

"I would arrange for a member of the staff to give you a tour, but I sense that you just want to be left alone. Am I correct?" Philip asked.

"Yes. Thank you for your kindness." With that, Unity rose from her chair and walked out into the Timber Ridge School. Later, as silently as she had arrived, she left. No teacher came to the office to report a strange woman in the building. She wasn't seen leaving the school. The only proof that she had been there was that Harriet, Philip, and Randy had seen her and talked with her.

"What did you make of the woman visitor?" Harriet asked with a slight shake of her head.

"I really don't know. She was different. Different in her peaceful presence, her few words that, when spoken, were kind and to the point. She had instant rapport with Randy. Her disappearance was as unnoticed as her arrival. I feel like I really didn't have the experience of meeting Unity this afternoon. It was like I took a short nap. It seems like a dream or maybe just my imagination," Philip said in a serious tone.

"Oh, no. She was here. No question about that. I didn't take a nap, and I know that I talked with her and brought her to you. I think she's just different as you say. I doubt that we will see her again. My guess is that she was embarrassed and didn't realize where she was. She wandered in here and visited for awhile. Plain and simple. She's gone and we won't see her again," Harriet predicted.

Chapter Two

A car pulled up to the Snow Castle Elementary School; a young girl got out and hurried up to the front door. She was probably late for school. Just before she got to the door, she looked to her right and saw a woman with a simple dress and a light jacket. The girl smiled and said, "Hello." The woman smiled back and raised her hand to acknowledge the greeting.

The girl went to the office to tell the secretary that she had arrived. The secretary, Linda Tolbert, smiled and said, "Good morning, Cindy. Your mom called and explained your tardiness. You may go on to your class."

"Thanks, Mrs. Tolbert. Who's the lady outside?"

"There's a lady outside?"

"She's standing by the front door."

"I'll go out and see. You go on to class, Cindy."

Mrs. Tolbert went outside the front door and didn't see anyone.

She thought it strange because Cindy was a polite and honest girl. She wouldn't have been one to lie to her; and, yet, there could only have been a minute from when Cindy entered the office until Mrs. Tolbert looked outside the front door.

When Mrs. Tolbert got back to the office, the internal school phone was ringing. "Hello."

"Linda? This is Les."

"Good morning, Les. What can I do for you?"

"There is a woman standing in the hall outside the sixth grade classroom."

"What's she doing?"

"She's just looking in the window at the children and Mr. Harris."

"Thanks, I'll be right down."

Linda Tolbert headed down the hall not sure what she would encounter. She had been the school's secretary for many years and from time to time an indigent person would wander into school. After all, the school was a warm place and the children were so adorable. Sometimes a grandmother will just come in to see the children and reminisce about her grandchildren who live in some distant state. Linda was sure that she would encounter a misplaced person, and, hopefully, she would be agreeable to leaving and would do so without making a scene.

"Good morning," Linda said, offering a warm greeting. The stranger smiled and acknowledged Linda's presence. "Can I help you?"

"The children are so adorable," the woman replied.

"Yes they are. Is one of them yours?" Linda asked.

"Oh, yes. They're all mine. Not in the way you mean; but, yes, everyone of them is special to me."

"They are special to all of us at Snow Castle Elementary School," Linda said, sounding quite proud of the compassion that the staff showed to the children. "Would you like to visit one of the classes for a few minutes?"

"I don't believe so. The children are always on my mind and they are with me," the woman said, exuding a sense of warmth and peace.

"Then why are you here?"

"I don't think you would understand. It's too early for my purpose to be known. But, I thank you for your kindness."

"If you don't mind my asking, what is your name?"

"My name is Unity."

"Oh, that's a pretty name. My name is Linda. Would you like to meet our principal, Mrs. Pelham?"

"Yes. That would be nice."

"Let's go down to her office. It's down the hall a bit."

"If you don't mind, you go ahead. I'd like to stay here for a few minutes. I'll come and meet the principal shortly."

"That's fine." Linda went to see Mrs. Pelham and to brief her for a different experience.

Unity watched through the window and smiled when she saw Brad in his wheelchair talking with another child. He seemed comfortable with what he was doing. She smiled when she saw a child share a book he was reading. Unity then turned the door handle and stepped inside. At once there was a calm and peace in the room. Brad, as well as the other children, stopped what they were doing and came to Unity. All felt as one in her presence. The teacher was in awe of what was happening. He had had many visitors to his room, but never had anyone brought such peace and joy simply by being present.

Unity smiled and touched each child as if giving a blessing. She smiled at the teacher and then turned and walked toward the office for a meeting with Mrs. Pelham. When she arrived, Betty was waiting to take her into Mrs. Pelham's office. The principal smiled and greeted Unity with a nod and a friendly hello.

"Thank you for coming to Snow Castle, Unity," Paula Pelham said with her hand out stretched for a greeting.

"It is my joy to be with the children in a place where they are comfortable and where there is love," Unity replied.

"Why thank you for such a nice compliment and kind words. Why did you come here? And, what can we do for you? Paula asked, inviting Unity to sit down by motioning toward a chair.

"This is where I am to be for a short time today. I came here to see the children and to receive their blessings. What can you do for me, you asked? You can accept me. You can allow me to share in the love that I find here; and, finally, you can welcome me back to be a part of the love."

Paula really didn't know what to say. She had entertained hundreds of visitors in Snow Castle and not one of them had a mission like Unity's. Not one had brought such peace and joy with their presence. "You are always welcome in this school," Paula said. The two women smiled and each felt a togetherness that could not be described. Paula turned to find some information about the school to give to Unity. When she turned back, Unity was gone.

"Linda," Paula called out nervously.

"Yes."

"Did you see Unity leave?"

"No, she was with you."

"I know, but I turned to get some information about our school and within a few seconds she was gone."

"I didn't see her come out of your office," Linda remarked, astonished that someone could simply disappear.

"Well, she couldn't have just disappeared into thin air. I was talking to a woman here in my office wasn't I?" Paula asked, a bit confused.

"Oh, yes. Of course you were."

Chapter Three

A few days later, the Toboggan Run Middle School students were coming into the cafetorium for their noon meal. As would be expected, there was much commotion. Most students followed a routine which was to sit with friends, talk, and eat their lunch. When Johnny looked to his right he saw a woman sitting at his table. He did a double take since no adult had ever sat at his table, which was basically reserved for his three friends and himself. His friends; Larry, Emily, and Billy, were still in the cafeteria line and would arrive during the next five minutes. Johnny always arrived first to establish control over the turf. He brought his lunch to school and came to the cafetorium from his locker.

Johnny didn't know if this woman was a new teacher or maybe a new lunchroom aide. Whoever she was, he wondered why was she here and at their table? He didn't object to her presence. She seemed calm and pleasant. "Waiting for your friends?" Unity asked.

"Yeah. Are you new here?" Johnny asked to satisfy his curiosity.

"Yes. I came to see you and your friends."

"Did we do something wrong or something?"

"No," Unity said, reassuring Johnny that he had done nothing wrong.

Just then, Emily came to the table with a look of curiosity about her. She probably thought this woman was a relative of Johnny's or as Johnny had thought, a new lunchroom aide.

"Hello, I'm Emily."

"Hi, Emily, my name is Unity."

"Are you related to Johnny?"

"Not in the way you mean. I am visiting today."

"Visiting 'cause you're going to work here?"

"I'll be working here, but not in the way you mean, work."

Billy approached the table with the same curiosity that Emily had. "This is Unity," Emily said to Billy. "She's visiting our school today."

Billy smiled and managed a nod which served as his greeting. Larry came up to the table to round out the quartet that ate together everyday. He sat down and Emily once again offered an introduction, "Unity, this is Larry."

"Hi," Larry said as he turned his attention to his sloppy joe and dill pickle.

Across the room stood the cafetorium aide, Laura Cole, who noticed Unity sitting with some students. She thought this strange as she hadn't been told about any new help. She was usually briefed about any visitors coming to the lunchroom. The Principal, Jean Worley, was always good about letting her know who would be coming into her region of responsibility. Laura had standards for the lunchroom and the students knew it and seemed to respect her authority.

Unity and the Children

"Can we help you with anything?" Emily said to Unity. "Do you want some of our food? Do you want to know about our school?"

"Thank you for offering me some of your food. You are very kind. I know about your school. I may ask for some help in the future."

Emily was the outspoken one of the four children. This was also the case when she was at the school student council meetings. Emily was a natural leader and well-liked, too. "We'll help if we can, won't we guys?"

Unity blessed each with a silent prayer and touched each on the shoulder or the head. "Thank you for being kind. I will look to you for help soon."

The four nodded in agreement and continued to eat their sloppy joes, except for Johnny, who had his daily peanut butter and jelly sandwich. When Emily turned to ask Unity another question, she was gone. She left without a farewell. "Did you guys see Unity leave?" Emily asked.

"Nope. She was here a second ago," Billy replied, surprised that the woman left so quickly and quietly.

"Did you guys feel love coming from her the way she looked and talked?" Emily asked. "I mean, I guess it was love, I felt joy and peace. You know what I mean?"

"Yeah. It was strange, but I just felt calm with her here," Johnny said.

"Somethin' about her. I can't describe it. She was neat. That's all," Larry said, groping for words to describe her presence.

"Right," Billy agreed.

"Wonder what she needs our help for? Wonder when we will see her again?" Emily asked.

Just then the lunchroom aide, Laura, came up to their table. "Who was that lady that was here a couple of minutes ago?"

"Her name is Unity," Emily replied.

"What was she doing here? Is she a student's mother?"

"No. She said she was visiting school and hoped we would give her some help when she came back," Emily said, acting as spokesperson.

"I think we ought to go talk to Mrs. Worley about her. She seemed strange," Laura said, believing that the principal needed to know about this visitor.

Emily felt a need to defend. "She's a beautiful person. She was kind and loving."

"As I was sayin', the lady is strange and if you and I don't know why she was in my lunchroom, then Mrs. Worley needs to know she was here," Laura offered, establishing her authority and dominion over the lunchroom. "When you guys finish, we'll all go have a talk with the principal."

A few minutes later, the five of them were walking into Mrs. Worley's office. Laura began, "Mrs. Worley, there was a strange lady in the lunchroom talking to these kids. You didn't tell me about any guest today, and I was wondering if a visitor may have signed in. Did you authorize a lady to be in the lunchroom?"

"No one is visiting so far today. How did she get in there?" Mrs. Worley asked.

"I was sitting at the table waiting for these guys and I turned and saw her sitting next to me," Johnny said. "We talked a little, then Emily came to the table and she talked to her. Then Billy arrived and we talked to her for a couple of minutes."

"She's a beautiful person," Emily said. "She was so calm and peaceful. I've never met anyone like her."

"Did she say why she was here or what she wanted?" Mrs. Worley asked.

"She just said she wanted to visit the school and asked us to help her in the future," Billy replied.

"Help her with what?" Mrs. Worley asked.

"She didn't say," Larry offered.

"Well, no harm done," said the principal. "I think you need to be very cautious about talking to strangers and I know you know that. When she comes again, I want you to immediately come and get me. Understand?"

"Yes," Emily said, while the others nodded in agreement.

Richard L. Baldwin

Chapter Four

It was a cold day and the students at Northern Lights High School were in a hurry to get into school from their cars and buses. The student council meeting was off to an early start. Barbara Conrad, a junior and the president-elect, was calling the meeting to order. They needed to start on time because there was much to do in an hour, and the administration wanted student input on the recommendations for the commencement speaker.

While Rob Stephenson was calling the roll, a woman entered the room and walked to the table where the students were meeting. She sat in an empty chair. "Excuse me, Rob. We have a guest." Barbara turned to the woman and said, "Welcome to our meeting. Would you like to introduce yourself?"

"Thank you. My name is Unity." Once again she brought an air of calm and peace.

"Has the superintendent or principal sent you here to observe?" Barbara asked.

"No. I am here for your future, the future of all children and the future of your community," Unity replied.

Barbara had an instant feeling of love for her. "Would you like to speak to us or just listen to our discussion?" Barbara asked, trying to be respectful but realizing she had a meeting to move along.

"Today I would like to listen," Unity said.

Everyone on the council seemed attracted to Unity. Even Eric, who was almost always cutting up, interrupting, and acting more like five than sixteen, was listening and feeling, as were the others, that he was in the presence of a loving soul.

"You're welcome here," Barbara said with a smile. "We'll proceed with our meeting and will look forward to seeing you and sharing ideas with you later." She asked Rob to continue the roll call and they began to address a rather full agenda.

The council advisor, Mr. Traylor, was proud of himself for letting this happen as it did. It would be his style to intercept this stranger, ask why she was here and direct her out of the meeting or escort her to the principal's office, or at least challenge her right to be in the school. Visitors are expected to follow procedures and are not allowed to just walk into classes or into student activities. Mr. Traylor stayed in his seat and observed. To be honest, he too, felt her peaceful presence and sensed her love for the students.

About a half hour into the meeting, Barbara looked to where Unity was seated and realized that she was gone. She asked if anyone had seen her go and no one remembered seeing her get up and leave. This seemed strange in a small meeting and Barbara said as directly as she could, "There was a lady here wasn't there? I mean, am I seeing things or what? There was a woman who said her name was Unity and she was very peaceful and loving. Right?"

Unity and the Children

They all shook their heads and even Mr. Traylor commented that, of course, she was there, but he didn't see her leave.

Chapter Five

It was about this time that people began to talk about Unity. The first time she was mentioned was at a principals' meeting. Dr. Heather Hosford had a monthly breakfast meeting in her office. This was a tradition that began four years ago. The first thing she did as superintendent was to meet with the principals. She knew that they were important people who could motivate the teachers and staff. How they carried out their responsibilities to improve the educational outcomes for the children of Winterhaven was very important.

Heather Hosford was in her mid-thirties. She was highly educated, in tune with current issues, and offered a style of leadership that was respected by her board, staff, and the community. Heather was stylishly dressed, her naturally curly hair rested on her shoulders, and her petite frame contained a personality that exuded leadership.

The principals in the Winterhaven School District were Mrs. Paula Pelham at the elementary school, Mr. Andrew Ketcham at the high school, Mrs. Jean Worley at the middle school, and they always invited Mr. Philip Brewer from the Timber Ridge School because some of the students with disabilities who went to that school lived in the Winterhaven District.

Dr. Hosford asked her usual open-ended question, "Does anyone have anything to share?"

Mrs. Pelham said, "I do. We had a visitor last week in our school. Her name is Unity and she seemed strange, yet there was a peacefulness about her that was beautiful."

"Why was she visiting?" Heather asked.

"You know I still don't know the answer to that question. She said she just wanted to visit the school."

"Come to think of it, a lady by that name was at Timber Ridge for awhile, too, Paula. She just wanted to visit. Some of you know Randy. When Randy came into my office he seemed mesmerized by this woman and gave her a warm hug," Mr. Brewer said.

"My lunchroom aide, Laura Cole, told me about a strange lady who was sitting at one of the lunch tables talking with four students," Mrs. Worley offered. "The kids found her to be a very loving person."

"I didn't see or meet this lady. My student council advisor, Mr. Traylor, said she was in the council meeting and that Barbara Conrad handled the situation beautifully. He also indicated that Unity was very loving and peaceful," Andrew Ketcham, the high school principal, added.

Dr. Hosford listened and summarized, "We have a strange lady named Unity appearing in our schools, meeting and talking with our students. Where does she live? Who is she? What is her purpose in visiting? I don't mean to sound like an investigative reporter, but we need to get some answers."

"It's all so innocent, Heather," Jean said. " She isn't a threat to anyone. Everyone who has met her has said that she is loving, calm, kind, polite, and courteous. That's what makes her strange I guess."

"Well, that's wonderful. I don't mean to sound difficult and uncaring, but I need to get this into some perspective," Heather responded. "The next time she appears at one of our schools, I want to be notified so I can talk with her."

Mr. Brewer poured everyone a fresh cup of coffee. Dr. Hosford's secretary, Mrs. Eleanor Eberhard, interrupted the meeting by saying, "Excuse me, Dr. Hosford, but the president of the parent teacher organization, Mr. Thorp is on the line and wants to talk to you as soon as possible about a person named Unity. Seems children have been talking to their parents about her and he wants to talk to you about it. I'm interrupting because he has to leave on a business trip in ten minutes."

"Thanks, Eleanor. I'll talk to him."

"Good morning, Mr. Thorp. How are you?"

"I'm doing just fine. I'm sorry to interrupt your meeting, but I'm leaving for an out-of-state business meeting in a few minutes and I promised several parents I'd call you about their concerns. Apparently, a strange lady seems to be visiting, unannounced, at our schools. Her name is Unity."

"Yes. I'm discussing this right now with our principals."

"The parents I've talked with say that their children tell them she is a very nice person. We parents are not alarmed, but we are wondering who she is and why she's coming into the schools and talking to the kids. Is this a project you or the school board is supporting?" Mr. Thorp asked.

"No. There's no project. It seems from what I've been able to learn this morning, that this woman has come into each of our schools. She does talk to some students and a few staff have talked with her. The principals thought her presence was strange. However, they handled it fine."

"I see. Does she live in Winterhaven?" Mr. Thorp asked.

"I don't know. I've told the principals that the next time she appears in one of our schools, I want to be notified so that I can meet her and get the answers to your questions, as well as some of my own."

"Okay. Sounds like you're on top of this. I'll call the parents who called me and explain what you have shared. We may be getting additional calls, I don't know. The kids are kind of taken by this woman and the parents are curious and a little concerned with a stranger just being able to enter classrooms, council meetings, and lunchrooms. You understand, I'm sure."

"I most certainly do, Mr. Thorp. I'll call you as soon as I learn anything. Thank you for bringing the parents' concerns to me as soon as you learned of them," Heather said.

"You're welcome. Have a good day."

Heather turned to her administrative staff, "Mr. Thorp says that several parents are hearing about this woman and are wondering who she is and why she is coming into our schools. If any parents call you, please tell them that I'm looking into this and that there is nothing to be concerned about."

They all nodded. The meeting progressed and was adjourned. It was time for school to get underway in the small and quaint town of Winterhaven.

Chapter Six

Each summer the Winterhaven student councils have a week long leadership experience at the Wildlife Sanctuary. The sanctuary serves as a camp where school groups go for a week, once a year, to get acquainted with nature, and to work together to improve their schools. A specific goal is to help students obtain confidence in helping their peers become more involved in making their schools conducive to better learning.

This year among the twenty students attending the leadership session at the Wildlife Sanctuary was Randy from the Timber Ridge School. He would attend with the school nurse, Mrs. Sue Hickok, and his health care aide, Mrs. Kathy Wilson. Others making the trip were Brad from the elementary school, Emily from the middle school, and Barbara from the high school. None of these students knew each other when all twenty gathered at the middle school to board the bus for the fifteen mile trip to the sanctuary. There was an air of excitement as everyone gathered with their luggage, books, and camping gear. Several parents were there to say "Good-bye," as were a few teachers.

The bus ride to the Wildlife Sanctuary took about a half hour. When they arrived, the students took their belongings to their respective cabins and began to unpack and settle into their temporary home. Once unpacked, everyone reported to Pine Lodge for orientation.

The director of Wildlife Sanctuary, Mr. Edward Throckmorton, looked like he belonged in Yellowstone National Park. He wore a green outfit and a hat that looked like it belonged on a Canadian Mountie. Mr. Ed's task was to be very clear about the rules that must be in place and to assure an orderly week of fun and learning. Listening to Mr. Ed was comforting in that he established where everything was and when and where the meals would be served. He explained the agenda for each day which allowed time for recreation, reading, hiking, or just being alone in nature which is what he hoped many of the young people would do. Ed was of the opinion that young people are on the go so much that taking a few minutes to sit under a pine tree or to sit on the dock at the lake is very important. He thought children needed to reflect, ponder, and just have some quiet time.

Once the orientation was complete, the students were given some free time to acquaint themselves with the sanctuary and to rest. Barbara valued the quiet time. She decided to put on her hiking boots and walk the two mile long Green Trail. She didn't invite any of the other students to join her since she wanted to begin this week by herself, thinking of what she hoped to get out of the experience.

About half way through the Green Trail, a bench is nestled in a grove of pine trees. Approaching this bench Barbara saw Unity seated on the bench. "Hi!" she exclaimed. "What are you doing here?"

"It is where I'm to be," Unity said with a smile.

"What a beautiful place."

"Yes, it is. I love to be in nature. Being alone and silent are what I enjoy whenever I can," Unity said.

"Are you going to attend our camping week?"

"You and the others will see me often. This is where you will learn truth and where you and the others will become new and enlightened messengers."

"What do you mean?"

"It will all become clear. You'll be happy with what you learn and the opportunity to create a new consciousness."

Barbara closed her eyes and took a deep breath. She lowered her head as if in prayer. She listened to the birds and felt a slight breeze on her face. She opened her eyes and looked toward Unity to ask a question. To her surprise, Unity was not there. She wondered what Unity meant, but she always felt such a calm when Unity was near that she looked forward to their next meeting. Barbara completed her hike and rested on her cot before joining the first class in Pine Lodge.

———

While Barbara was enjoying her walk, Brad, in his wheelchair, had made his way to a deck which overlooked the marshlands. Brad had no brothers or sisters. He was handsome and trim with well developed muscles for a ten year old. Moving his chair for the past few years no doubt made him quite strong. He was often seen smiling and his personality was delightful. Brad's disability was the result of an automobile accident when he was eight years old. His teacher reports that Brad is quite intelligent, charismatic, popular and is considered a leader at Snow Castle Elementary.

Brad was looking out at the marsh. He watched the birds, flying free and searching for food. He knew that he had that same freedom in his mind and in his imagination. He knew that he could not physically enjoy movement like his friends, but he could imagine. With his mind he was able to do everything that anyone else could do. As he watched the birds flitting into and out of tall pines, and moving gracefully against the blue sky, he sensed someone near. He turned and saw Unity standing to his right.

"Hi Brad." Unity said cheerfully. "Beautiful creatures, aren't they?"

"Hi, Unity," Brad responded happy to see Unity once again. "I fly with them. Sometimes I imagine being beside them when they fly, dive, and, land."

"The mind is a wonderful thing. We can be anywhere, do anything, and experience whatever we wish just by using our minds and imaginations."

"My mother taught me that my mind has no limitation. That even though my legs are paralyzed, I'm only limited physically, but not mentally."

"Your mother is a wise woman."

"Are you going to be at camp all week?" Brad asked.

"Yes, I'll be here often," Unity replied. "I have work to do here. I'm hoping you'll help me."

"I will if I can."

"People have been misdirected for a long time in their ideas about the differences in people. They are confused," Unity said, sitting next to Brad, looking into his eyes and touching his hand. "Together we can enlighten them. I know you can be of help to me and to thousands of other children who are limited in some physical way but who are equally free in the use of their minds. We will teach them."

Unity and the Children

Brad knew what Unity meant. He watched a bird take off, soar, and go through quite a set of maneuvers before alighting on the branch of a tree. He looked to his right, Unity was not there. He was anxious to see her again.

———

Emily sat on her cot and opened her diary. She was pretty and very intelligent. She loved playing the oboe, playing soccer, and cataloging beanie babies. She thought that keeping a diary would help her practice her writing and would also help her focus on some of her feelings. She was alone in her cabin when Unity walked in and sat on the bed next to her. Emily was glad to see Unity and gave her a hug as she said, "Oh, it's so good to see you again."

"It's wonderful to see you too, Emily."

"Are you going to be with us all week?"

"I'm always with you, but, yes, I'll be with you often during the week. We've a shared responsibility that will bring us much joy this week and for weeks and years to come."

"What are we to do?"

"You'll know at the appropriate time. You'll be filled with joy."

"I'm writing a diary. I'll write that you are here and sharing the week with us."

"Your diary will help you reflect on your ideas and what you're learning. It will be a friend as I am a friend."

Emily turned to get her diary and pen which had fallen on the floor. When she looked back, Unity was gone. She must have slipped out the door when another student came into the cabin to get a jacket. Emily felt such peace whenever Unity was with her. *Oh, that she could be such a friend for another,* she thought.

———

Randy and Sue, his nurse, along with Kathy, his aide, were over at the flower garden enjoying some sunshine when Unity joined them. Sue and Kathy welcomed her, "Hello. Do you work here at the sanctuary?"

"Not in the way you mean work. I'm joining some of the children this week, yes."

With the sound of her voice, Randy looked up, smiled and as at Timber Ridge School, he reached up to give Unity a gentle hug. "Hi, Randy," Unity said.

"Randy can't talk very well. He uses a computer," Kathy replied.

"Randy talks, but he doesn't talk like we do," Unity replied.

The nurse and the aide looked at each other and exchanged confused glances.

"Randy is severely disabled," Sue said.

"Randy is spirit and isn't able to carry out his thoughts and actions as others do, but he communicates and radiates with great joy," Unity said with assuredness. "His spirit soars in love. You just don't think you can see or feel it."

"His disability limits his communication, his mobility, and he rarely smiles," Kathy added.

"He smiles whenever his soul joins mine. It appears to you on the physical level that he is different. On the level of spirit, he's no different than you or me. He will be of help to us this week and well into the future."

"I'd like a few minutes alone with Randy," Unity said to Kathy and Sue. "He'll be fine for a few minutes without you."

"We'll take a short walk and be back," Sue said, as the two of them began to stroll near the garden.

When it was time for Randy to go to school, there were few opportunities in the public schools for meeting his needs. He was placed in a separate school and it wasn't until the advent of technology that people began to understand that Randy was capable of high-level thinking. His family decided to continue his education at Timber Ridge because he was comfortable at the school, and he could receive a concentration of services in one building.

"Your disability is a beautiful characteristic of your personality," Unity said to Randy. "You know that your spirit is connected to me and to everyone. There is no separation. The separation people see is an illusion. I need you to help people see the connection so that they can look beyond the judgment and fear they have when their senses tell them you are not connected. Do you understand?"

Randy typed into his computer, "LOVE CONNECTS."

"Yes it does, Randy. It certainly does."

Sue and Kathy came back to join them. When they arrived, the Pine Lodge bell was ringing. Both women looked in the direction of the bell. When they looked back at Unity, she was gone. "Who was that?" Kathy asked.

"I don't know. She was so calm and peaceful."

"Yes, but what was she talking about?"

"I haven't a clue. You think she's on the staff here?"

"Mr. Ed didn't introduce a person named Unity. I think we need to mention her to Mr. Traylor," Sue said. "I've never heard anyone say those things. We did talk with a lady didn't we? Or, did we just imagine it?"

"Oh, no. She was with us. Did you notice Randy all the time she was here?" Kathy asked. "He seemed to follow whatever she was saying and he smiled when she talked. I've never seen him act like that around anyone, have you?"

"No, I haven't."

After lunch the twenty students were divided into five groups. Their responsibility was to plan and develop a project that they would complete during their week. Barbara, Brad, Emily, and Randy heard their names read as the third group of four. Each group was composed of at least one person from the elementary, middle, and high school. In addition, each group had a teacher assigned who was to monitor the group's progress. Ted Traylor was assigned to the third group. This pleased him because he had such respect for Barbara and the way she led the high school student council. In addition, the nurse and the aide who were with Randy were also to be a part of this group.

Chapter Seven

Each group was assigned to a table in Pine Lodge to begin its work. Barbara asked Mr. Ed if they could go outside to the garden. They could hear better there and being in nature would inspire the group to be creative. Her request was granted and the seven proceeded to the flower garden. Ted, Sue, and Kathy picked up a picnic table and brought it to the garden. When all had assembled, Barbara spoke. "First of all, let's find out who we are and introduce ourselves. My name is Barbara and I attend Northern Lights High School."

"My name is Emily and I go to the Toboggan Run Middle School."

"I'm a 5th grader at Snow Castle Elementary School," Brad offered.

Randy typed his name into his computer. Sue looked at the screen and said, "This young man's name is Randy. He goes to the Timber Ridge School. I'm Sue, the nurse at the school."

"My name is Kathy. I'm Randy's aide."

Ted Traylor was known by most, but in a spirit of cooperation he said, "I'm Mr. Traylor from Northern Lights High School." Ted was tall, balding, and a bit overweight. He truly loved being with young people. Some people are perfectly situated in a profession. Such was the case with Mr. Traylor.

"This will be a good group," Barbara said, feeling upbeat and positive about the members in her group. "I have a feeling that we'll enjoy working together. As you heard, we need to come up with a project for the week. We need to plan it and to carry it out. Any suggestions?"

Emily spoke, "I suggest that each of us go to a quiet place and think of an idea. In about fifteen minutes we would come back together and share."

"Good idea. Any comments or suggestions?" Barbara asked.

Ted wanted to interject his thoughts, but held back realizing that this was to be a student driven activity.

Randy seemed to be nodding but perhaps it was just random movements that were common with him. Brad said, "Maybe she's right; a little time to think would be a good idea."

"Okay," Barbara said. "Let's take Emily's advice. Mr. Traylor, would you round us up in fifteen to twenty minutes?" He nodded that he would. "Everyone can either stay here and think or go elsewhere. When we get back together, we'll discuss any ideas we have and go from there. Good idea, Emily. Let's have some quiet time to think."

Barbara strolled over to a large oak tree. She sat at the base of the tree and began to think. She closed her eyes to concentrate. Her thoughts were interrupted by Unity. "Barbara, it is time for you to expand your consciousness and become a leader in your school and your community. Your vision will eventually go beyond your community to your state and your country. It is time. Listen and I'll help you grow. It's no accident that Brad and Randy are in your group. They are present for your growth and you're in the group for their growth."

"In what way am I to grow?" Barbara asked.

"Action was taken many years ago that was well-intended and had to happen in the evolution of assistance to people with disabilities, but it's time to move to a higher consciousness and you are being chosen to lead this journey."

"Why me?" Barbara asked.

"You're receptive and kind. You're a leader among young people. The change that's needed will occur with children and young adults. It's too late for the adults to make the change. They can intellectually desire a change, but their way of thinking is rooted in separation. You and the others are not rooted. Your freedom can take people to a higher consciousness and to a better society."

"What has been rooted in separation?"

"Many years ago children with disabilities were not accepted in schools. They stayed home with their parents or they were placed in institutions. If they did go to school, they were singled out and perhaps ridiculed. States established schools for the deaf and the blind and children were placed in institutions for the retarded or for the severely disabled. People didn't think they could learn. Often people were embarrassed to have people with disabilities in their communities.

"People eventually came to the realization that children with disabilities had a right to an education just like all other children in the community. Being a society of laws, the political leaders passed legislation that required what is called special education to be provided for children and young adults who were disabled."

"Like Brad and Randy?"

"Yes, like Brad, Randy, and all the students at Timber Ridge and schools like Timber Ridge all across this country."

"This is wonderful, isn't it?" Barbara asked.

"It has provided opportunity. It has allowed people with disabilities to go to school, and to remain at home with their families. So, yes, Barbara, it is wonderful. However, the movement to provide all of this opportunity resulted in continued separation. Now, you have a chance to work with students to make a change that is needed."

"What do you mean, 'continued separation?'"

"The laws led to separation, to disunity, to pulling people apart, instead of coming together."

"I still don't get it."

"The law was designed to give students with disabilities the same opportunities students without disabilities have to go to school. But it also reinforced the perception of separation. The law and its regulations separated people. It led to children having labels, teachers dividing up the children, and funding going to separate programs. People were taxed for separate buildings, and laws and rules were developed that only applied to certain children and families. Policies were created that treated some people different than others. This separation led to jealousy, anger, frustration, bitterness, conflict, and many hurtful situations. What was such a dream come true is today a false promise. Our current reality often lacks love, respect, dignity, and unity. We don't need the laws and the rules, Barbara. We need unity and from unity we will have respect and dignity. We can't undo what has happened, but we can start to undo all of the separation."

"What can I do?" Barbara asked, a bit overwhelmed by the responsibility of reversing much tradition.

"You can plant the seeds to start people thinking of doing things differently. To date, the emphasis on changing attitude has been focused on special education teachers changing the attitudes of other teachers and students. What is needed is for children to lead the attitude change."

"Will you always be there to guide and direct me?"

"You have never been alone, Barbara, and of course, I'll always be with you to guide and support you," Unity said reassuredly.

"Have you talked to others about this?" Barbara asked.

"Yes, and I'll be working with Emily, Brad, and Randy as well as with Mr. Traylor to help you and others."

Barbara took a deep breath and closed her eyes pondering what all of this meant and what would change in her life because of Unity's presence. When she opened her eyes she was alone. She stood up and made her way back to the garden to join the others.

When all were back together, Barbara asked if anyone had any ideas from their quiet time. "I think all of the student councils should set aside a day each year to celebrate our differences," Emily offered after a short silence. "There are students in Winterhaven who represent a variety of cultures and I think it would be fun to have a day where kids wear outfits from their native countries. We might eat food from other cultures too."

"That's a great idea, Emily. Good job." Barbara said enthusiastically. "Brad, what did you come up with?"

"I thought our project could be something to do with the environment. Maybe we could sponsor a cleanup day in Winterhaven."

"Another great idea. Good work, guys! I wonder what Randy came up with?"

Randy typed on his computer, UNITY.

"Good thinking, Randy," Barbara said with a smile. "Boy we sure could use more of that."

"What did you think about, Barbara?" Emily asked.

"I think that we should do something in our school district that would lessen the separation that has been happening for many years. I agree with Randy. We need to develop unity in our schools."

"What do you mean, Barbara?" Ted replied, unable to contain his thoughts any longer.

"I think that treating some people differently for so long has caused everyone to believe that our differences are more pronounced than our similarities. In giving people privileges, we separate them from others. In treating people differently, we develop emotions that cause jealousy, anger, and bitterness. This isn't good for our schools, community, state, or nation," Barbara said, surprised by her eloquence.

"What project would you suggest, Barbara?" Sue asked.

"I think that we should unify Winterhaven."

"That's practically impossible," Kathy quickly interjected. "People are people. The emotions you speak of are common human emotions. You're talking about a perfect world. You're thinking of doing what religions have failed to do for centuries."

"Well, I suggest that we think of all this over lunch. We can decide this afternoon. We should be in agreement and we should have a strong sense of what we want to do and how we will do it. Maybe my idea is too pie-in-the sky. Maybe we should tackle something that's concrete and not so controversial."

As the people were leaving the garden, Randy got Barbara's attention. She looked at his computer screen and saw, "YES." Randy smiled as she looked at him. They both turned to look toward the lake and there on the dock stood Unity. She was smiling and they felt her calm and peaceful presence.

Chapter Eight

Barbara thought it best to have a talk with Mr. Traylor. She would need his support here at the sanctuary and back in the real world of Winterhaven. After lunch she suggested they walk along the Green Trail as she wanted to talk with him.

They talked first about the weather and what a great place the sanctuary was for getting away from it all and reflecting on important things. "What's on your mind, Barbara?" Ted asked, as they came to a meadow where a turnout offered a magnificent view of flowers, trees, and grasses.

"Because I trust you and your ability to let me go with my ideas, I thought it best to share some experiences and thoughts."

"Thank you for your trust. You're a wonderful leader. It's a joy to watch you work with others, Barbara."

"Thanks. Soon after we arrived, I took this hiking trail to relax, enjoy the trees, and to be alone. I met Unity once again and we talked about the importance of this week's leadership meeting."

"Unity is here?" Ted asked.

"Yes. She's wherever I am and wherever you are if you want to have her in your life."

"Superintendent Hosford is becoming concerned because parents are asking about this woman and wondering why she's appearing in our schools."

"I can understand that. People have a hard time with anything different in their lives, especially when the person or event doesn't conform to their expectations of what should be happening. But, yes, Unity and I have talked twice since we've been here and I know she has talked with Emily, Brad, Randy, Sue, and Kathy."

"What's she saying or telling you?"

"She's bringing us an awareness. She believes we can be a force to change attitudes."

"This is exciting, but a little scary, Barbara. People are going to rebel when they learn that Winterhaven students are talking to a woman named Unity who just somehow magically appears and disappears, and who is influencing our young people to change attitudes."

"I can understand that, Mr. Traylor, but I believe in what she tells me and I think we need to try to change our attitudes about educating people with disabilities."

"Change in what way?"

"Well, Unity has explained that in having many laws and rules to protect people with disabilities, we have, in reality, taken steps to isolate them and to separate and divide us."

"She has a point," Ted replied. "It seems that the laws to assure children like Brad and Randy an education have led to labels, to excessive paperwork, to meetings, and to costly confrontational experiences between parents, school leaders, and government agencies."

"I think I understand the separation. We feel like we are separate because what we see are differences," Barbara said.

"Yes. This separation between students, teachers, and administrators, has led to a system of education that doesn't promote cooperation. It leads to people separating themselves into segments of the educational community like general education and special education, disabled and nondisabled kids. There is money for some children and money for other children, special equipment for some but not for others," Ted said, reflecting on his years in the schools and working with children with disabilities.

"My special education colleagues have told me that it has brought people from the consolidated district, the state, and the federal government into our schools to monitor if we are following the laws instead of looking to see if we are coming together to serve all the children in an equitable way. It has led to paperwork being emphasized as being more important than talking together about what is best for all students. It has led to tax dollars being used for people to serve people with disabilities instead of a shared use of dollars for the benefit of all children."

"We even have separate schools for people," Barbara said, remembering what Unity had told her earlier. "We have a special school for Randy and others. Some students with disabilities have special transportation that isn't any more special than transportation provided for the rest of us except that their buses have lifts."

"Yes. And they have special education meetings all the time, one per student plus an evaluation meeting and other meetings to discuss a variety of topics that should be discussed by everyone," Ted added, with a hint of the frustration he'd been experiencing as a teacher. "The system is fractured, but the students it serves are not fractured. Our children are very together, needing each other to grow, not needing to be separated by labels, systems, or funding. All the students of Winterhaven need to have adult guides who can see the value of our coming together in unity."

"Well stated," Barbara said, impressed with Mr. Traylor's eloquence. "It seems to me that we are thinking that some change may be needed."

"Yes, I guess we are," Ted stated, a bit taken back by Barbara's conclusion. "We must not lose sight of what we learned from special education; good evaluation of strengths, individualized planning, accommodating the disability, and adjusting curriculum to learning styles, which, by the way, should be standards provided for every student in Winterhaven."

"I agree. I think we need to reverse the separation and celebrate our connectedness."

"You put forth a convincing argument, Barbara. I'll help you even though I think you and the group will have a tough row to hoe, not so much out here in this isolated environment, but when we get back to Winterhaven. We'll also have to work together to explain Unity. Seems like unity and dismantling separate systems are two very difficult items to contend with, wouldn't you agree?"

"Yes. But we've got to try because it's the right thing to do."

"I agree," Ted replied, nodding his head. "I hope I can meet Unity sometime. She seems like a beautiful person."

"She is and you can't help but feel loved when you are with her. Thank you for understanding, Mr. Traylor. You are kind of rare yourself. Not many advisors would be willing to stand up with students and take some risks with them. I have a feeling that we may be starting something that has much good in it."

Barbara and Ted continued their walk and arrived back at

the garden feeling refreshed from the hike. They were ready to tackle a project that would certainly cause a stir, to put it mildly, when school resumed in late August.

———

When the group reconvened, Barbara said, "This morning we decided that we might want to have a project that would change some attitudes in Winterhaven. Have we thought of something better, or shall we go ahead?"

"I like it," Brad said enthusiastically. "I want to be accepted for myself. I like what everyone is doing to help me, but I just want to be Brad."

"Try to explain it, Brad," Emily said.

"Physically I'm different from others, but inside I am not different. The love that I feel is the same love that you feel. This doesn't have anything to do with whether legs move. Everyone has differences, and wouldn't it be neat if we had a school where our differences were celebrated."

"That's what I mean," Barbara said. "Brad said it so well. We're the same love, but what we see physically, we judge. We decide to laugh at someone, to talk about someone, and we approach or stay away based on our judgments of what we see and experience. If we focused on the love that equalizes all of us, we would have no need to judge others."

"I think we should talk about how we can change things," Emily suggested.

"What do you have in mind to change?" Barbara asked.

"Well, for one thing, I know that there are kids in my school who have problems learning, and instead of staying with us in the classroom, they leave and go to a special education classroom for awhile. Others go somewhere to get help with their reading or math. It seems to me that those kids could stay in the classroom and learn with us. Or, the special education teacher could come into our room, and not only help children with learning problems, but anyone who may need a little extra help."

"I agree with that," Brad said with feeling. "I learn in the special education class. My teacher is good, but why do I need to be in two different rooms?"

"I know," Barbara replied. "In the high school the same thing takes place. Kids are shuffled here and there. I'm not sure it all makes sense. Like Emily said, why can't we handle the differences in learning in one classroom? There must be creative ways to reach people that don't require children getting a label or going to special rooms."

"I have to comment," Kathy interjected, feeling some frustration in what she was hearing. "You kids just don't understand. Students like Randy and Brad are special. They have a right to special opportunities with teachers trained to meet their individual needs. Randy goes to a special school that's designed for him. He's happy there with other students who have disabilities." The students and Mr. Traylor listened respectfully.

"Why?" Barbara asked.

"Why? Because, these kids need special environments, special teachers, special administrators, special forms, evaluation teams, and special equipment."

Once again Barbara asked, "Why?"

"I told you. These people are different. They need different classes, teachers, buildings, equipment, curriculum, forms, meetings."

"I don't think so," Emily said. "If we realized that we are connected we wouldn't need all the different things you mentioned."

"Do you mean to tell me that Randy is not different from other teenagers?" Kathy said, becoming quite agitated. "Look at him."

Unity and the Children

"We are having a discussion here and not a debate," Barbara said feeling the emotion. "There is no need to get angry."

"I'm not angry. You kids just don't understand."

"I think we understand," Barbara remarked. "We just don't understand what you want us to understand."

"I think you're wasting everyone's time. We came out here for a leadership conference, not to throw out an important part of our school system. Leadership is not destroying what we've had in place for a long time, especially when what we've had in place has helped so many kids and their families," Kathy said, with intense emotion.

"I think leadership is like getting up in the tallest tree in a forest and looking out beyond the trees to the valley. The leader then helps people on the ground move through the forest to the valley," Barbara explained her leadership analogy once again. "As some of us look out from the tallest tree, we see a unification of the systems where children aren't labeled, aren't put in different schools, or shifted around a building to different teachers for different periods of time."

"But, just putting kids like Randy and Brad in your classrooms will be like going back to the '50s or '60s," Kathy added. "They will not get what they need."

"We wouldn't propose that Brad and Randy just be placed into our classrooms," Barbara countered. "Placement into a class doesn't assure learning even for Emily or me. The unification involves support because without support, you are right, we'll be back to a time in our history that we don't want to revisit. The secret is providing support for everyone in the school."

"Do you think you can replace all of the special teachers, therapists, aides, administrators, psychologists, social workers, physical and occupational therapists that work with Randy and other students?" Sue asked.

"No," Emily replied. "But, we can teach, support, involve and assist all of them."

"If you didn't have a Timber Ridge School, where would students like Randy get their physical education? Put on their plays? Have their assemblies? They have a special swimming pool. The therapists have plenty of room for their work," Sue reminded the group. "You can't duplicate this school in the other Winterhaven schools."

"Maybe, if many children at Timber Ridge go to their neighborhood schools, some classes could be established for other children there," Emily suggested. "Maybe Timber Ridge could be used for technology or for some purpose to serve all students?"

"Perhaps it could be where the district sets up a communications center," Barbara added. "These are good ideas. Can you imagine all of the other ideas if people just stretched their imaginations a bit?"

The afternoon meeting progressed with much discussion between Barbara, Brad, and Emily and with an occasional message from Randy. Ted thought they were working well together. He was proud of the dialogue between Sue, Kathy, and the students. They would be needing to face the critics many times. They could use some experience handling tough opposition. Anytime change is presented, it is the human condition to resist. There's comfort in the status quo. The children were coming up with some revolutionary ideas for change that would affect everyone in Winterhaven.

Ted excused himself from the group. He decided to take a walk to reflect a bit about these ideas. After all, he would have to defend and support the students. He would need to talk with Dr. Hosford, principals, and school board members. He felt he needed a little quiet time to think this through. He decided to walk the Red Trail which was only a mile long. He would be back in about twenty minutes. About five minutes into his walk, he noticed a figure in the distance. As he got closer, he could tell that it was Unity. She was waiting for him at a deck looking out on a small pond where turtles sat on a protruding log in the pool of clear and calm water.

"Good afternoon," Unity said.

"Hi." Ted replied, as he came up to her and shook her hand.

"We finally meet. I saw you at the student council meeting. You're fortunate to have Barbara leading that group."

"She's very talented. Well, I'm pleased to finally meet you," Ted said sincerely. "You're certainly bringing new thinking to the children."

"It's time. And it's time for you to be a helpful guide."

Ted could sense the peace and love that came from being in Unity's presence. "What's my role?" Ted asked.

"The children will be the force of change, and it must come from them. But, they must be guided and you'll be able to point the way. You'll have the wisdom to be their friend and their rock when they need a stable guide."

"I'll do all I can, but please help me understand. I've been listening and trying to be supportive, but I'm finding myself listening to Sue and Kathy. I see the separation and its effects, but I'm not sure there is the problem that the children and you see."

"I can help you since you're ready to receive truth," Unity said preparing to teach Ted. "People think they are separate, but they're not. All people, and in fact, all of life, is connected. When people use their senses, they perceive that each person is apart from each other. When the perceived differences are not consistent with what the people have been taught to be normal, the ego or self 'tells' the person that this difference is not to be valued or celebrated. The differences are seen as an impairment, or people functioning differently. Unfortunately, people have learned to pity people with disabilities. The outgrowth of this thinking is to put out, leave out, or discard, and what follows is treating people differently. This separates people even more and exaggerates the differences they already perceive themselves to have."

Unity continued to teach. "All that I have described is not natural. Not living naturally leads to a lack of unity between everyone, because in reality, even though people can't 'see' it, we are all the same. What we think about one another, is really what we think about ourselves. What we do to another, is what we are doing to ourselves. What is natural is to be unified in love because we all are the same. We are all love. Like so many paradoxes, while we appear to be different, we are the same. People can't understand this, because they believe their senses and don't trust their spirituality.

"Once people can get beyond the brain's belief that what is seen is separate from themselves, they begin to see that love connects. Love has no eyes to perceive a difference. Love has no brain to interpret a difference. Love has no ego to make sure that the person protects himself or herself from what is different. Love is the equalizer. Love is what breaks through the ignorance, and the five sense impression that most people depend on for their decisions and actions. The students have this love, and they are letting the love govern their thoughts and actions. It is love that will follow them to Winterhaven, and it is love that will change people's hearts. This will in turn create a new way of doing things; and, as you will see, love will guide people to a celebration of the connection between all people.

"Also, diversity will be valued. In loving diversity, the need to separate will disappear. When separation disappears, unity will be present and the unity of souls is love because as you will learn, all there is, is love. It's all that exists. Anything that is not love is not real. It seems real to the brain and the ego, but to the soul, whatever isn't love is an illusion. Each person is created to live in love and living in love is to be free of illusions, feeling connected to all."

This was a lot for Ted to comprehend. He had listened carefully and followed what Unity told him. But, it would take some thinking to fully grasp what he had heard. "I think I'm beginning to understand. I hope you'll be patient with me. You gave me quite a bit to think about."

"You'll continue to understand, Ted. Watch, listen, and follow the thinking of the children and your growth will be evident."

"I'll do my best to understand."

"Your understanding is so that you can guide the children. They will teach the people of Winterhaven. You, understanding connectedness, can be their friend and their support."

"Yes, I will. I'm thankful for your teaching." He glanced back on the trail as he thought he heard someone coming. When he looked back, Unity was gone. He continued to feel an energy field that could only be described as loving and peaceful. He walked back to the group knowing that he was no longer the same man he was when he started out on the Red Trail several minutes ago.

—◆—

Ted pulled up a chair and continued to listen to the discussion. It was going well. All of a sudden Barbara said, "I think we need a break. Everyone agree?" Each nodded. "All of this thinking tires the brain. Let's take some time for ourselves. Then, we'll come back together for a few minutes before we have some fun. I think Mr. Ed said we'd be free for recreation about three-thirty."

Sue and Kathy pushed Randy in his wheelchair, and they went to the Lodge. Brad, in his wheelchair once again, went to the deck to watch the geese and other wild birds. Emily went to her cabin to write in her diary. Barbara felt a need to once again take a walk. Ted stopped her. "You're doing a great job as always."

"Thanks. This is fun. I enjoy it when people expand their minds."

"I talked with Unity."

"Isn't she wonderful?"

"I have never felt so loved and so much at peace in my life."

"I know." Barbara said, obviously pleased that Ted had met and talked with Unity.

"Barbara, I think I understand what needs to be done. Unity has taught me. I now know my role. The change will come from you and the others. I'm to be a friend and to offer support. I want you to know that I'll be there for you. I've a sense that all will go well, because love will guide us. We'll be okay as long as we follow love instead of believing the illusions which are products of our senses and our mind's interpretation of what it receives."

"I know. I also know that everything will be given to us to accomplish the goal. This isn't to say that we won't have many hurdles along the way, but I know that whatever we need will be given."

Chapter Nine

One of the other high school students at the sanctuary came up and gave Mr. Traylor a message that read, "Please call Dr. Hosford as soon as possible."

"I've got to call Dr. Hosford." Ted shared the message with Barbara and said, "Maybe this will be the first test of your words that 'Whatever we need will be given.'"

The phone rang twice before Dr. Hosford's secretary, Eleanor, answered, "Superintendent's Office."

"Hi, Eleanor, Ted Traylor returning Dr. Hosford's call."

"How's your leadership conference going, Ted?"

"We're off to a good start. Thanks."

"Good. I'll get Dr. Hosford."

Within five seconds he heard, "Ted?"

"Yes. How're you Dr. Hosford?"

"I'm fine. How're you and the students getting along?"

"So far, so good. I got a message that you called."

"Yes, I did. I received a call from Phil Brewer at the Timber Ridge School. He had received a call from Sue Hickok who is with, I think the student's name is Randy?"

"Yes. Randy is here representing the Timber Ridge School."

"Okay. Anyway, she told Phil that the students in your group are planning to do away with special education when they return from the leadership conference. I told him that there had to be some mistake, and that I would call you and find out where such a rumor came from."

"I'm glad you called. I didn't know that Sue had called Mr. Brewer. I was going to call you, but I didn't think it important at this point. I guess in retrospect I misjudged that. I'm sorry."

"No problem, Ted. You mean there may be some truth to this?"

"Yes. The students in my group are thinking that separation needs to be replaced with a unification in Winterhaven."

"What do you mean, Ted?"

"I'd like to suggest that you come out to the sanctuary. I think it would be better if I could talk to you in person, and that you listen to what the children are saying. You can't help but be impressed with their thoughts and their ideas for making our school district more responsive to all children."

"I suppose I could do that. I'm looking at my calendar, and I have the whole afternoon clear tomorrow. How about my arriving around one-thirty and staying for a couple of hours?"

"That sounds fine."

"Okay. I'll see you then. Is there anything else I should know?"

"About an hour ago I met Unity and it was a beautiful experience."

"She is out there?" Heather asked, with an air of disbelief.

"She is and she has been talking with the students too."

"Can you arrange for me to meet her? I've got to find out who she is and why she is talking with students and coming into our schools."

"I can't arrange a meeting, Dr. Hosford. She decides who she talks to as best as I can determine. If I see her before tomorrow, I'll tell her that you wish to see her."

"Okay, thanks, Ted. Call me if you feel that I need to know anything during the week. Call me at home if you think it necessary."

"I will. All will be fine. I have no concern. The students are discussing social issues and you will be proud of them when you talk with them tomorrow. I'll tell Barbara, who is the group leader, that you will join them for their afternoon session."

"Thanks, Ted. See you tomorrow."

Ted caught Barbara a few minutes before the group reconvened and told her about his talk with Dr. Hosford. He told her that he thought it wonderful that the superintendent was coming out to listen to the discussion. He also told her that Dr. Hosford was wanting to meet Unity, except that she was looking for answers to why Unity is coming around to their schools and talking to Winterhaven students.

Barbara called the group back to task. "Mr. Traylor told me that he has talked with Dr. Hosford. She has decided to join us tomorrow afternoon. I think this is great. We can share some of our ideas with her." The other members of the group smiled and nodded.

Sue felt especially pleased because she was sure that the superintendent would see the craziness in all of this talk of unification. She felt confident that Mr. Brewer took steps after her call to get to the bottom of this nonsense and it apparently worked. Sue was certain that Dr. Hosford would listen to what was being said and then politely put a stop to these ideas."

"Before Dr. Hosford gets here, I think we should plan what we will say," Emily suggested.

"We need to support our ideas," Brad added. "We can't talk unification and then think separation."

"Good point, Brad," Barbara offered. "Let's put down what we believe and see if our discussion and thinking has brought us to a focal point."

"I think we should have a set of principles that will guide whatever plans we develop," Emily said. Again, except for Sue and Kathy, there were nods of agreement.

Ted quietly asked Sue and Kathy to leave the group for a few minutes as he wanted a few words with them. They walked toward a picnic table under a large oak tree. "I know that you're not accepting what the students are thinking," Ted said cautiously, not wanting to sound judgmental. "I know this from your comments, your body language, and your call to Mr. Brewer. I think it's fine for you to have your thoughts, and ideas, and opinions, but..."

"Ted, you know, as do we, that this is all such a waste of time. These kids can't stop a system that has federal and state law behind it and has been in place for thirty some years," Kathy said.

"Why do we let them keep talking about this," Sue added. "As adults, I think we have a responsibility to guide them to something realistic. Brad suggested an environment day where students could clean up the school grounds or the river bank going through town. Now there is a project that's worthwhile, not stopping a tried and true way of helping kids with disabilities."

Ted was patient. He listened and said, "I think a leadership conference like this is to allow our students the opportunity to think and to discuss matters of interest to them. You and I know that the school district is run by a board of education elected by the citizens of Winterhaven. You and I know that the parent teacher organization has much power in school policy. We know that teachers and principals are key players in what happens in the schools. I see no harm in having these young people talk about change. I think we should encourage them. They are wanting greater acceptance of people with disabilities and we all know that this would be desirable. So, I'm going to ask you to be supportive and not to offer critical comments. I think we should challenge their thinking and help them understand some implications of their thoughts. But, I would hope that we can support them in their ideas no matter how idealistic or unrealistic we might think them to be."

"I guess you're right," Kathy said after a few seconds of pondering Ted's comments. "We're only here to care for Randy. We're not on the student councils and we're not employees of the Winterhaven School District. I still think they're wasting time, but I can see that our role is to assist Randy and not to interrupt the students' activity. Thanks for talking with us. It helps." Sue nodded in agreement. The three walked back and quietly joined the group.

By this time the students had identified four principles and had them written on a large pad of paper hanging on an easel. The three adults read independently,

Principles for the Unification of Winterhaven

1. *Our differences are perceived by our senses. We are in fact connected and are part of one another.*
2. *Any system, procedure, words, or activity that reinforce separation must be dissolved.*
3. *If any procedure, process, or activity is good for one, it is good for all.*
4. *We celebrate our differences as they remind us that we must support each other at all times.*

"Do we agree on these?" Barbara asked. All agreed that these four would be a good basis for a plan to unify Winterhaven.

It was time to end the first day of the leadership conference. A lot had been accomplished in a few short hours. The group had agreed upon a project. They had identified four principles upon which to guide their thinking and recommended activities. They had secured an audience with the superintendent even though it was not by invitation, but by her request to get to the bottom of a disruptive concept to some. The students broke for recreation, dinner, and a movie in the evening. Tuesday would be here before long.

Chapter Ten

Following breakfast and some announcements from Mr. Throckmorten, the groups were to gather for continued discussion. Barbara's group decided to work in a corner of the lodge because the rain was coming down gently, prohibiting any outdoor work.

"Okay, as I recall, we left off yesterday with four principles," Barbara reminded the group. "Since we've all had time to think about this for a few hours, does anyone have a change to suggest?" The students were silent and by their silence, indicated agreement. "Good. We have a few hours before Dr. Hosford joins us. We should probably use this time to decide what we'll say in support of our project," Barbara explained.

Randy who had been surprisingly attentive, at least that was Kathy's perception, got the attention of the group by typing the word "PLAY" into his computer. The word appeared on his screen.

"You mean put on a play to express our ideas?" Barbara asked.

Randy seemed to nod approvingly but nonetheless typed, "YES."

"Any support for Randy's idea?" Barbara asked.

Emily was first to respond. "I think it's a great idea. It's creative and entertaining and might be a good way to get our points across." Others nodded.

"Okay. Let's put on a play!" Barbara said enthusiastically.

"I think Barbara should play the part of Dr. Hosford. I could be a teacher," Emily said. "Brad could be the principal and Randy, Mr. Traylor, Mrs. Hickok, and Mrs. Wilson could be students in the class."

"Does anyone have a better idea?" Barbara asked.

"I think Mrs. Hickok should be the narrator like a radio announcer," Brad suggested. "You know kind of like, 'Today we are visiting Winterhaven School District where we've learned of a new way of thinking.'"

"I like that," Sue said being supportive. "Sure, I could be the roving reporter." Ted smiled. He was pleased to see the nurse who called Mr. Brewer to report a major threat to the system now playing a part in a drama to impress the superintendent of the need to think differently. "Miracles do happen," he thought.

"Okay. I'll play the part of the superintendent, Emily will be a teacher, Brad will be the principal, Mrs. Hickok will be the media reporter, Randy, Mr. Traylor, and Mrs. Wilson will be students. Wait, I suggest that Randy play the part of the PTO president, Mr. Traylor will be the president of the Winterhaven School Board and we'll have Mrs. Wilson and Dr. Hosford play the part of the students," Barbara summarized.

"Great," Brad said and others agreed. The cast was set. Emily wrote each person's name and the part they would play on the flip chart next to the four principles.

"Now, let's talk about the script," Barbara suggested.

"As the roving reporter, I suggest that I set the stage for the play," Sue said. "Maybe make it like a television story of about fifteen minutes, kind of like the major networks do. You know, 'Here we are in Winterhaven where some students are changing attitudes. They have proposed the acceptance of all students, and the provision of a quality education at the same time without, I might add, resorting to a common system that we know as special education.'"

"Great introduction, Mrs. Hickok. I like that," Brad said while others smiled and nodded affirmatively.

"Then what would happen?" Barbara asked.

"I think the students would talk to the superintendent and explain our new way of thinking," Emily said.

"But, one of the students in our play is Dr. Hosford, and she doesn't know what we're thinking. How could she play the part?" Barbara reminded the group. "Don't we want her to watch the play? Maybe she should be in it, but be an observer?"

Ted finally thought of an idea that he could interject. As Unity had said, he was to be a friend and a guide. "I think it's good to involve Dr. Hosford in the play, but I think some of us should brief her for a few minutes so that she can be a participant. We learn by doing, and having her involved will cause her to become a part of the drama and the change. So, I'd suggest we leave the cast as is, but have the play about two-thirty. Then, after Dr. Hosford arrives, we'll be able to talk with her about your ideas."

"Everyone agree with Mr. Traylor's suggestion?" Barbara asked. Again her suggestion was met with positive head nods. "Okay, what do the students say to the superintendent?"

"I think we just explain that we value being connected instead of separate," Brad suggested. "Then we give some examples. We'll suggest a better way that would be good for everyone in the school district."

"Okay, and I think we should explain how an attitude shift will lead to doing things differently," Barb added. "Then we could give some examples."

"Next, I think the superintendent and the students should talk to the presidents of the school board and the PTO," Brad suggested. "Maybe taking them to the Winterhaven Cafe for lunch. Finally we need to talk to the principal, and then the teacher."

"Right. Then we'll go back to the roving reporter who will summarize the experience," Sue suggested. "I think we've enough confidence in what we've been talking about that we can just wing it. We may want to do a quick dress rehearsal after lunch before we talk with Dr. Hosford."

With that, they all felt ready to introduce their new thinking to the superintendent.

Chapter Eleven

Dr. Hosford woke up early on Tuesday morning. Her routine was predictable. She got the morning paper, which arrived before five, and read it hoping not to see criticism of the Winterhaven School District. Ever since she was appointed superintendent, she read each edition with the hope that the reporting would be fair, and if positive stories couldn't always be told, then at least, she hoped, they would be truthful. She read the paper and prepared a light breakfast of cereal, toast, and orange juice. She got dressed and rounded up her papers and materials to take to her office.

While driving to work, she had a feeling that she should pull into the city park. The morning air was warm and there was no wind to speak of. She didn't understand the urge to go into the city park, but she did, thinking that maybe it was a good idea to appreciate the rose garden and the hundreds of flowers that were in the community garden. People had often told her that she needed to slow down and smell the flowers. Sometimes her life seemed so hectic that the seasons flew by. Before she knew it, summer would be over and the trees would be turning into their annual change from green to various shades of red and gold.

Heather parked her car and got out. She decided to take a stroll through the garden. Because it was early in the morning, there was no one in the park. She wasn't in a hurry to get to the office. Her day was expected to be quiet, with an afternoon visit to the Wildlife Sanctuary to meet Ted Traylor and the students at the leadership conference.

Heather strolled past all the flowers reading the nameplates that gave the species and genus of each. She enjoyed the aroma and the silence while sitting on a bench to take some deep breaths and to meditate for a moment or two. She had not taken a quiet moment like this in quite awhile. It felt good. She thought that she needed to get back to this practice. Heather closed her eyes and soaked up the peace and beauty that was all about her.

When she opened her eyes and prepared to go to her car, she saw a woman standing in the rose garden. As she walked past the woman, she heard, "Heather?"

"Yes, I'm Heather Hosford. Do I know you?"

"My name is Unity. It's good to see you again."

"Have we met before? I'm sorry, I don't remember."

"Yes, we have on many occasions, but I understand that you do not recognize me."

"Unity? Are you the person who's been visiting our schools and talking to some of our students?"

"Yes. I am."

"I've been wanting to meet you and to ask why are you're doing this?"

"It's time for me to do so. The children will lead you and

others to a new understanding that we are all one, and that our separateness is an illusion," Unity said.

"What do you mean 'our separateness is an illusion?'"

"I think the children will explain this to you this afternoon. As an introduction to their activity, I'll say that for too long we have believed that we are not connected. Our senses 'tell' us that we look different, act different, and we use this information to make judgments about what we see. It's these judgments that reinforce differences, because we come to believe in an undefinable concept called normal.

"We use information from our senses. The brain interprets this information to judge what isn't normal and in that judgment we separate from each other. The truth is that we're all connected and we're all one. There is no separation, we only think there's separation. Once we realize that we are all one, we begin to embrace and learn from our diversities. We accept and love. We find no need to judge, categorize, label, separate, discriminate, alienate, and put distance between us. This is the lesson of the children. They're seeing that we're connected and seeing this, they have a new understanding that doesn't fit with the world that is being presented to them."

"What world?"

"In school, they see separateness all about them. They see some children who are given labels, who are expected to go to other rooms, who are given some privileges because of their perceived difference, who are seen by a variety of adults who have special meetings, use special forms, and who follow special procedures all because separation is dominant."

"I'm beginning to see what you mean. They're looking at each other as connected, and seeing this, they can't 'see' what makes them different."

"Yes, because in reality, they're not."

"But, the differences are real."

"No, the differences are an illusion. The only thing that is real is that which connects all, and that is love."

"That's nice to say, Unity, but the young people are different in hundreds of ways. Each has a unique personality, each has a different learning style, each comes from a different family situation, and I could go on and on," Heather said.

"What you say is the product of information processed by your brain based on information given by your senses."

"Yes, but it's the basis for how we live and conduct our day-to-day lives."

"Yes it is and that's the change that is needed. We are living by the illusions and not by the truth. If we could live by the truth, the day-to-day lives would be without illusions and judgments."

"What does this all mean, Unity?"

"This means that from the children will come truth, the understanding of connectedness. The children will be free of the illusions, and as they teach and model truth, others will come to this awareness. Then the awareness will grow to acceptance, and the separation will cease. Unity and connectedness will have replaced separation and all the pain and inappropriate thoughts and actions that stem from this immature and erroneous perception."

"But how will this new thinking lead to meeting the needs of our students?"

"What will be different is the motivation of the activity to help others. Now, the source is the perception of difference and its resulting separation. What the children are thinking is that the source of their perceptions is love and a connectedness. When you act on the perceived differences, you find that people reach out to people from pity, from a need to help people who are not, as people say, normal, who are different from themselves. This is a level of compassion that is admirable, but the children are acting out of a knowing that love is the connecting force between all. When this is their reality, they reach out to help another because they know that in helping another they are helping themselves."

"Do the children expect us to work within the laws and rules for special education?"

"There's no need for rules or laws when the truth is perceived. You only need laws and rules when people perceive separation. If you act out of love which binds all, you don't need a governmental force to control behavior. The behavior will be natural and the behavior will have love at its source. People who operate with laws and rules are in a state of fear. Laws and rules are symbols of separation. Love replaces fear. When love is dominant, the help comes to people as a natural extension of compassion for another because it is the same compassion one has for him or herself."

"I'm sensing that I have a role in this change. Am I correct?"

"Yes, Heather. You do, and the children need your support to lead people in truth. You're the leader of the educational community which the children see as a microcosm of the community. They need you to allow them the opportunity to express their new-found wisdom and truth."

"How can I help?"

"They need you to support them when they teach their peers, their teachers, principals, parents, the school board, and the PTO. I will assure you, Heather, that accepting this truth will allow everything that you need to be there for you. You cannot fail nor can you find anything other than a presence of peace and calm about you. A new you will be sensed by all who come into your presence."

"I feel that love, peace, and calm with you, Unity. I think I understand, but I sense that I understand with my intellect and not with my heart."

"Yes. You're right. You don't know of what I speak at this time. You'll eventually arrive at this knowing, but it's all a part of your growth and your journey. You do know that some of your students are understanding truth and will act from love. They will plant some very important seeds in your school district. What they need is a leader to prepare the soil so that the seeds may take root and produce good fruit."

"I'll support them. Will you be there for them and for me?" Heather asked.

"I'm always in the hearts and minds of everyone. The children have a knowing that love is with them. You can have that same knowing, but only you can decide to become one with this truth."

Heather heard a car honking a horn and she turned to see if someone was trying to get her attention. When she turned back to continue talking with Unity, she was gone. This couldn't be since she was beside her a couple of seconds ago. Heather quickly wondered if she was having an hallucination. After all, what was she doing in a city park on a workday morning? Maybe her meditation had led to a short nap, and she had been dreaming. No, she had not been dreaming. She was talking with a woman who was full of love and peace. Heather also knew that much of the dialogue was mental and not nearly enough from the heart. She did know that she was to help the students and not be a force that would inhibit their desire to change attitudes.

She couldn't help thinking that she was in for several confrontations with people who probably wouldn't understand. But, Unity spoke truth. She knew that the words she had heard were universal truth. While she couldn't fully understand how this truth would be manifested, she knew that what was coming had to happen for it would represent a significant change in human interaction.

Heather walked to her car and drove to the office. She spent the morning going through her paperwork and making several calls. She couldn't help but ponder Unity's words. She also knew that she retained everything that Unity had said, and she realized that she was unlearning all the illusions that had been her life for all of her thirty-five years. Finally, she realized that she had a choice and the choice was to follow her knowing or to follow the perceptions of her senses. She was listening more to her heart, and she had a sense that she was on the brink of a knowing.

She was anxious to get to the Wildlife Sanctuary and to learn from the children. *Learn from the children,* she thought. *I should have known that the truth would come from the youngsters, not from the adults, the administrators, the teachers, the parents, the community leaders, or the state and federal government. The truth would come from the students, the truth being that we are all connected by love, and in this connection we are all one.*

Back at the Wildlife Sanctuary the students were taking a break from their planning session for the afternoon meeting. Before they came back together, Barbara had an intuitive thought that the four students should meet without the three adults. So, when they reconvened, Barbara said, "If it would be all right with everyone, I'd like to suggest that Randy, Brad, Emily, and I meet by ourselves for a few minutes."

Ted responded, "Of course, this leadership conference encourages students to talk, plan, and learn independence." There was a picnic area several yards from the lodge. The soft rain had stopped and left the air fresh and clean. "I suggest you meet over in the picnic area. It's quiet there."

"Thanks. Good idea," Barbara said.

Barbara and Emily walked over to the area. Brad turned the wheels of his chair and followed close behind. Kathy pushed Randy in his wheelchair, and when she was assured of his comfort, she left to rejoin Sue and Ted who decided to have a meeting of their own in anticipation of Dr. Hosford's visit.

"I thought the four of us should meet," Barbara began. "I think we're on the verge of an adventure that will test us. We'll need to be strong and confident. We'll be leaving this safe place, ironically called a sanctuary, to go into a world that is based on separateness and that is filled with people who are not believing that all are connected by love. These people will reject us just like Mrs. Wilson did, and the reality of what we'll face is that everyone will be thinking like her and will have trouble understanding us and our knowing."

Randy got everyone's attention and on his computer screen they read "FOCUS," and it was an encouraging message to keep focused on the truth. The truth would prevail. It would strengthen them in times of challenge.

Brad said that they should develop a belief statement which could be their anchor. It would do what Randy suggested - serve to focus and give them strength.

"This is a time for Unity to be with us," Emily said.

"She is," Barbara said with assurance. "I can feel her peace and her calm in our sharing and in our knowing. She has helped us understand the truth and each of us knows this and what it means. Yes, Emily, it would be nice to have her sitting with us in this picnic area, but we also realize that she's with us always in our knowing. All we need to do to have her with us is use our minds to bring her into our thoughts."

Barbara continued, "Let's take Brad's suggestion to develop a belief statement." They nodded and began to think. After about a half hour, the statement was complete. It read;

Unity and the Children

Beyond what our physical senses perceive, which is a world of separateness, is our knowing that we are all connected by love. Knowing that we are connected leads to unconditional love which results in kindness and compassion and service.

Each of the four students carefully read what they had created. Randy typed into his computer, "IT IS SO." The others smiled and felt very good about what was put forth. Emily said, "Unity was with us when we developed this, I know it. I didn't see her with my eyes or hear her with my ears as I have before, but I heard her in my heart and in my mind. I felt the same love and peace as I do when she is physically with me." Each understood what Emily was saying.

While the students were meeting in the picnic area, Ted, Sue, and Kathy were talking among themselves. Sue said, "I hope all of this works out. I want to protect them from people just like I want to protect Randy. The world is so cruel and it will be so to these young people. They are talking about change and change that's so foreign to people. I don't want their ideas to crash on them. They're so delicate and vulnerable."

"I know what you mean," Kathy replied. "I also know that children need room to fail. This will be a learning experience for them just like other experiences. They'll present their ideas and the people will be kind, perhaps, but nothing will change. Special educators and Dr. Hosford will listen politely. They will allow the children to comment before the school board and the PTO, but beyond that all will remain as it is. But, like you, I hope they don't get hurt or have their self concepts damaged. Young people as well as adults can be so cruel and they'll be laughed at and made fun of. But, as Ted said, we need to support their ideas. So, we will, but I hope they don't get hurt."

"I've worked with young people for almost thirty years. I've seen the energy go to so many issues as young people grow and mature," Ted remarked. "But, this issue I think will take hold, and I believe it will be positive for Winterhaven." Their conversation turned to small talk until they saw the students coming from the picnic area to the lodge.

The seven mingled and talked about the weather, and what a nice week they were having. The camp bell rang for lunch and everyone made their way to the lodge for the noon meal.

Chapter Twelve

At about one o'clock, Heather Hosford pulled into the Wildlife Sanctuary. She parked and followed the signs to the lodge. She spotted Ted who was talking with Barbara. She walked up and gave each a firm handshake stating that she was glad to be out in the beauty of nature for an afternoon. "Thanks for taking some of your valuable time to meet with us," Barbara said with a smile. "We know that you'll be open to our suggestions and we appreciate your support and advice."

"Maybe it would be a good idea for the three of us to talk for a bit before the whole group gets together," Ted suggested. "I think you'd like to be briefed. You'll probably be hearing some suggestions that would create quite a shift in how students are being served. Maybe hearing a little from us would ease you into the afternoon meeting."

"That's fine. I'm here till about three-thirty and whatever you wish to do during this time is fine with me," Dr. Hosford responded. "I do have a sense that I would like to spend some of the time just talking with the students."

"Absolutely, I think that's a fine idea," Ted said.

"Why don't we go over to the picnic area and have a talk," Barbara suggested. "It's quiet there and we won't be disturbed." They nodded in agreement and the three walked to the same spot where the students had gathered earlier in the day.

"Before we begin, I should tell you that I met Unity this morning. I was on my way to work, and I had a feeling that I should stop at the city park in Winterhaven. I was taking in the peace and quiet and enjoying the fragrances when I noticed her. We had a conversation before she disappeared. So, I have been thinking quite a bit today about what she said."

"We've all had the experience of meeting Unity and learning from her," Ted said with a smile. "Her message is with each of us. It seems to me, we need to integrate what we have learned into our lives. It's one thing to understand the truth, and another to live it."

"Yes, it is and what you'll learn this afternoon is that Emily, Brad, Randy, and I are wanting to bring Unity's message into our school community."

"I realize that, and I'm hoping I can understand what you have in mind to accomplish this. What I learned this morning from Unity is that the truth will come from the children. What I have yet to learn is what all of this means. I need to understand this so I can guide or at least predict where all of the problems are going to be."

Barbara said confidently, "There won't be any problem we can't work through."

"That would be your hope I'm sure, but from experience I know that change is always problematic. No matter what is suggested or proposed, some people will object to it, fight it, or set up barriers, and as you know Barbara, it is often the students who are good examples of this."

"I think there will be people who don't initially understand what is happening, but at the same time the change we speak of will be natural because we'll be moving from an unnatural practice to a natural one. We've set the goal, and when a goal is set, the rest follows smoothly."

"Talk to me about the change, Barbara."

"We believe that the current system of educating children with disabilities is unnatural because the activity is rooted in seeing each other as separate."

"But, the students are disabled and we've a state and federal obligation to serve these children with special education," Heather replied.

"We perceive the children as being disabled because our senses send signals to the brain which the brain interprets, and this sets off separatist thinking and activities. All of the government requirements stem from the separation-difference model. Just calling it 'special education' tells you that it's a separate system, and once separate, we fall into the unnatural way of serving."

"Barbara, why don't you present what's natural and maybe that will help us see another way," Ted suggested.

"Yes, maybe that would help," Heather replied.

Just then Brad approached the three in the picnic area. All three greeted him, shared what had been said so far, and asked him to join them for the remainder of the discussion. Barbara began and just before she was to offer her idea, she sensed Unity's presence. She offered a quick silent thought that Unity would guide her thoughts and words. A peaceful feeling filled her as she said, "The change, or what is natural, is to see the truth, that we are all one. We're connected and not separate as our senses perceive us to be. It's like this: our senses 'tell' us that the earth is stationary, that the sun rises, moves across the sky and sets in the evening. Our senses also 'tell' us that the earth's surface is flat. We know that the earth is moving through space; the sun is stationary and the earth moves around the sun; and that the earth is round. So, if we believed our senses, we would be very ignorant.

"It is the same with our perception of people. Our senses tell us that we're different because we perceive the physical body and note through judging that there are differences. For example, Brad can't walk, Larry Williams's skin is a different color than mine, Mr. Traylor is a man, et cetera. If we just believe our perceptions, we think we're different and thinking this way leads us to judge, separate, and treat people differently. What Unity's message to the us is, is that while we are unique in many ways, we are one and what connects us is love. Once we understand this, we accept and enjoy unique differences."

"Okay, I think I understand. Go on."

"Once we understand that we are not separate, we change what we do. We act out of love because we realize that we're really responding to ourselves. I don't label Brad because in so doing I label myself. I don't have pity for Brad, because to do so would be to pity myself. To stretch it a bit further, I am not the physical body my senses tell me I am. I'm spirit, and it's in this understanding that I know that Brad is spirit. The spirit we share is love, and in being love, we are connected. Since we're connected, we embrace and learn from our diversities because at our core, we are one."

"Precisely. Great explanation, Barb!" Brad said.

"I think I'm beginning to understand. Wow! I think I've just seen a picture of earth from space and it isn't flat!" Heather said in wonder. "What a teacher you are, Barbara! Let me take this from here and see if I've got it."

"Please do," Barbara said.

"So, in school, we may not need a separate system because we are not separate. We are operating from a separate-different mentality instead of a connected-one mentality."

"That's right," Barbara said with Brad, Emily, and Ted nodding.

"Okay, I've got that. Now, how does that change what we do?" Heather asked.

"Well, first of all we have no need to label," Brad said.

"I know, but the law says..."

"We're not working from law now. Law is in the world of separateness. It was created because of a separateness mentality. Everyone saw people with disabilities as different, judged them as different, treated them as different, and then passed laws which assured they remained different," Barbara said.

"But surely this was good for children and their families," Heather said confidently.

"Once again, the people perceived it as good because they perceived separateness. When one views people as separate, then all of these practices; labels, laws, policies, et cetera follow and fit so nicely into their perception of reality. Back to your question, 'Was this good for children and their families?' Yes, if you view it from perceived separateness and, no, if you view it from connectedness. Because we see connectedness, we don't see a need for the law."

"I see. Go ahead."

"Helping each other flows from love," Brad continued. "What we do for another person, we do for ourselves. So, now we can see that all of us want to help each other. We don't want a friend sent down the hall to a separate classroom. But, it's okay to spend time with a specialist to learn in some other setting. It's okay, because through love, you want everyone to learn and to grow.

Anyone can receive individual attention from the specialist in any setting. Therefore, we move in our thinking from someone going to a special education classroom to a school having a learning center where anyone can go. Do you see the difference?"

"Yes, I think so and not only that, it's a great idea," Heather replied with enthusiasm. "What you're doing is unifying our district. You're helping each other out of love and making all resources available to everyone because we are all connected."

"Absolutely," Barbara said, pleased that her superintendent was understanding and sounding supportive.

"How does this affect our diagnostic team?" Heather asked.

"After a shift of perception occurs, there's no effect. We still need to know how we learn. We still need help in adjusting to the world. We still need the various therapies. This new thinking doesn't clone us all into one learner. So, even though connected and one, we maintain our unique personalities. It is just that we now act out of love for ourselves and we embrace and learn from our diversities.

"There would be one change, however, the diagnostic staff and counselors would be there for every student in Winterhaven, not just special education students," Barbara continued. "Now, it seems that the school psychologist just evaluates students who may be eligible for special education or who are in special education. The same with the school social worker, speech and language therapist, occupational or physical therapist, and audiologist. These people would serve all within our school district. You see, simply put, the unity exists throughout the school. Anybody can get help from anyone and anybody can go to any activity or setting that will benefit them or where they can benefit another. There are no more barriers: no barriers with words, systems, environments, policies, or practices."

"But, the government won't understand."

"You're right. They may understand, but they can't act on their understanding. You see, their entire system is built on separateness," Ted explained. "The laws and rules they must implement and administer, the forms they use, the procedures they follow, the data they collect, the dollars they provide. It's all based on separateness."

"I understand, but we need money for the unification of Winterhaven. So, how will we shift our thinking and thereby our activity and still maintain a separate system to get money and assure compliance with our state and federal laws?" Heather asked, a bit frustrated with her desire to accept change but needing the current resources to serve all of Winterhaven's students.

"That's a challenge, but Unity will help. If you ask her to help with that, she'll do it," Brad said.

"We hope this discussion has been helpful," Ted remarked. "We're supposed to join Emily, Randy, Sue, and Kathy for a group discussion, and I think the students have a surprise for you."

"I don't know if I can handle any more surprises today. Since getting up this morning, I've met Unity and I've been introduced to a new way of thinking which is causing me to see a different way of serving the children of Winterhaven. What a day! Where are we going next?"

"Let's go meet the rest of our group," Barbara said. The four of them made their way to where Emily, Randy, Sue and Kathy were enjoying some time sitting in the sun; soaking in the silence and beauty. Introductions were made and everyone seemed comfortable with each other.

"Have you been having a good week?" Heather asked.

"It's very exciting to think, share, and imagine what can be," Emily said. Randy got everyone's attention and when they looked on his computer screen they read, "VISION." Emily smiled, touched him on the shoulder and said, "Absolutely. When we think, share, and imagine we create vision. The vision eventually happens."

"Why don't you share your vision with me," Heather said, thankful for her introduction a few minutes ago.

"We will and we look forward to doing this on two levels. We'll share it here at the sanctuary, and with your support, in our schools this fall," Barbara said.

"I'm ready. Let me see what you've come up with in the last day or two."

The students provided the performance and their message of connectedness and how their new thinking could be implemented in their schools. Dr. Hosford gave the children a standing ovation when the skit was over. The two women, Sue and Kathy, were still a bit skeptical, but they were beginning to see what was happening. There was a transformation going on and they felt comfortable, even though they'd bet it wouldn't fully take once school opened in the fall.

Ted experienced bliss realizing what the students had done, and how their change of thinking was helping others understand a whole new expression of compassion. He was proud of them and he knew that it would be a challenge, but he would experience much joy working with all of the children and the teachers in the school district.

"Before I go back to work I'd like to have a few words with the students," Heather replied. The three left the group and the superintendent and the student council representatives from each school were together.

"Well, we've quite a journey ahead," Heather said.

"It'll be exciting," Emily offered.

"We'll teach others," Brad added.

Unity and the Children

Barbara noticed that Unity was approaching. They looked toward her and their souls were filled with joy in anticipation of her presence.

"Hi, Unity," Barbara said. "Thanks for joining us. We know you're always with us spiritually, but having you physically present is very special."

"The joy is also mine. You're doing a wonderful job accepting the new responsibility you have."

"We've quite a task before us, Unity," Heather replied. "I don't think many will understand this new way of thinking. I'm afraid that most will laugh at us, turn against us, and we'll not be successful."

"All will be fine. You've expressed a fear and fear is not what truth is about. You said, 'I'm afraid...' and that thought alone separates you from love which is all that really exists."

"Yes, but I have a school board who expects special education to be in place for the students with disabilities. Mrs. Willis is on the board and she has a child with a disability. I have teachers who expect eligible students to go to a placc whcrc they will get special instruction by teachers and aides who have knowledge and skill to handle their learning differences. I have a parent-teacher organization that is rightfully skeptical of anything suggested. Of course I'm afraid. I'll be laughed out of town and may even be the laughing stock of superintendents all across the state," Heather said with much frustration.

Unity stood before the group. She lowered her head as if in prayer. After several seconds, she lifted her head, and with all listening came these words, "You now have truth. You now have love which conquers all. You now have no fear of failure, because when you live in truth, and think, and act with love, you'll accomplish miracles.

"When you return to school this fall, you won't be laughed at, you'll be seen as leaders who brought divergent systems into one. You, Heather, will be seen for what you are, a leader who listened to the children and offered them support in changing a separate system into one of unification. I want to emphasize this. You, Dr. Hosford, are not leading this change, the students are. Dr. Hosford will only facilitate the work of the students. Notice that the children did not say they were afraid or concerned that they would be laughed at or scorned by others. It was you, and it was your thought of self that caused you to comment. You were concerned how others would think of you.

"The children with their new way of thinking do not think of self without thinking of all. They do not envision judgment of another, so they cannot see others judging them. They realize that they are connected to the school board, PTO, teachers, and students. When you're connected, you don't laugh at yourself, and you don't fear yourself. The children will teach and other students will learn. Soon thereafter, parents, teachers, and school board members will come to see that separateness and a lack of connectedness are not natural, are not love, and are not truth. Quite the opposite will happen, Dr. Hosford. Winterhaven will become a center for creativity.

"Your biggest problem will be scheduling visitors who will hear of what's happening and will come to see what the students have taught. Before I leave you, know that everything you need will be given to you. Words to say, people to act, support for each other, it will all be there in abundance. If today you have any doubt, you will encounter a number of instances when you will see this truth. As I leave, please know that the children know the truth, and in living the truth, they will have no fear, and they will have everything they need to accomplish bringing unity to Winterhaven."

Unity and the Children

Unity disappeared. The group sat silently for a moment thinking on her words and feeling the calm, the peace, and the love that was present.

After a few moments, Dr. Hosford spoke. "This has been a marvelous afternoon. I thank each of you for your leadership, your love, and your desires. I'll do whatever I can to help you do what you must do. You'll have my door open to you. You can know that whatever you need from me will be there for you." Each student gave her a warm smile and a hug. Randy typed into his computer, "THANKS." Dr. Hosford walked toward her car. Mr. Traylor, Mrs. Hickok, and Mrs. Wilson could be seen talking with her briefly before she drove away.

Richard L. Baldwin

Chapter Thirteen

Before Heather was out of the Wildlife Sanctuary, she picked up her car phone and called Eleanor. "Superintendent's Office."

"Hi, Eleanor. I'm leaving the sanctuary and will be at the office in about a half hour. Please contact Mr. Thorp of the PTO; our principals; Mr. Brewer; the school board president, Mrs. Meredith; and the head of the teachers' union, Mr. Ludlow. I'd like to have a breakfast meeting with them on Monday morning. Hopefully they all can be there. This isn't much warning, but I expect most will be able to join me."

"Okay. Do I tell them what this is about?"

"Oh, I suppose they'll want to know why I wish to see them together. Tell them I want to introduce them to the most exciting school year in the history of Winterhaven. That ought to heighten their curiosity."

"I'll handle it, Dr. Hosford. I imagine you'll want to meet in the board room? I'll order the food. Is eight-thirty okay with you? Nothing is on your calendar for Monday morning."

"Yes to all of those questions. Thanks, Eleanor. I'll see you soon. Good-bye." Heather was refreshed and ready for the children to lead her and others to a change that would be full of challenge and wonder. She smiled and had a sense that Unity was smiling, too.

Back at the sanctuary, the students had gone to their cabins to prepare for some recreation. They had had a very challenging day and were off to a great start. They had the support of their superintendent. They had a sense of mission, and their play helped them focus on the task ahead. It was time for a swim or some volleyball. Dinner would follow and then an evening of fellowship with other school leaders. A movie with popcorn was the scheduled entertainment before retiring and beginning again on Wednesday.

Wednesday and Thursday were days devoted to planning what they would be doing once the school year began. With Ted's support, the children continued their discussion and talked about activities they would use when school started. Unity met with the children on occasion and by the time the week leadership conference was complete, Barbara, Emily, Brad, and Randy were ready for the change that was theirs to begin and enjoy. Before the students left the sanctuary, Dr. Hosford called and asked them to attend the Monday morning meeting.

Barbara, Emily, Brad, and Randy would have another month and a half before the beginning of the school year. They all agreed to meet in each other's homes at least once a week. Mr. Traylor was invited, too, and he made a special point to attend each get-together. After all, he was to be a guide, a friend, and a support to the students.

———————

On Monday morning at precisely eight-thirty, several people were gathered in the board room of the Winterhaven School District. A continental breakfast was available for the persons invited to attend. Each took their coffee, tea, or juice along with fruit, yogurt, and a muffin. Seated around an oblong table with comfortable leather chairs, they noticed that Dr. Hosford was in a good mood. After all had a chance to eat, to greet each other, and to ask about how everyone's summer was progressing, she asked for everyone's attention.

"Thank you for coming to meet with me this morning. I know I didn't give you much notice, but each invited participant is present and I appreciate that. I felt it important to introduce a change that will be coming to Winterhaven. At the outset, I want to say that I'm fully in support of what I think will happen. I'm asking that you offer whatever support you can."

"If your intent was to arouse our curiosity, you have done a great job," Mr. Thorp said with a cautious smile. "I just can't imagine what would be coming, of a positive nature, that would cause you to bring each of us here this morning."

"I don't mean to arouse your curiosity, but being human I would imagine that each of you is wondering what's on my mind. I won't keep you in suspense any longer. Last week, several of our student leaders were at the Wildlife Sanctuary, attending our annual student council leadership retreat. The students were expected to develop a project and to implement it in the upcoming year. You may recall that in the past, our students began a recycling project that has been operative to this day. Another project a few years ago was to develop a healthier set of food choices for the snack bar and cafeteria. That, too, is still a matter of policy. This year, four of our leaders, Barbara Conrad of the high school, Emily Hernandez of the middle school, Brad Proudfoot of the elementary school, and Randy Lubienski of the Timber Ridge School were a team and they have developed their project for this coming year."

"I know each of those students, and Winterhaven couldn't

have picked a better set of students to work together," offered Mrs. Myra Meredith, school board president.

"With our support they will be implementing their project when school opens this fall," Heather said.

"What can we expect?" Mr. Ludlow, from the teacher's union, asked.

"What they will lead us toward, is a unified school district."

"Unified? We are that already, it seems to me. We work together. We've a community spirit. We've good athletic team spirit of working together. I'd say we are well unified now. What do they have in mind?" Mr. Ludlow asked.

"The students have had an attitude change which causes them, and I join them in this, to see that we are all connected in love. We are not separate, even though our senses 'tell' our brains that we are separate. In our perception of separateness, we judge, and in judging, we further separate ourselves from each other. We create separate systems like special education and other programs that are designed for specific students with special instructors, forms, dollars, procedures, et cetera," Heather answered. She could tell that the first set of nerves had been touched. Some began to use their body language to communicate a level of discomfort with what they were hearing. Heather thought, *Oh, Unity, be here with me.*

"Let's not begin to get into messy church and state issues," Mr. Ludlow suggested.

"This isn't about religion, Mr. Ludlow. This is about people treating others with respect and dignity. This is about embracing our differences instead of judging others because of them. I'm very sensitive to religion and not crossing that important line between what education's role is and the role of the family, and the community's religious institutions," Heather said with assurance.

Unity and the Children

"Let's just let Heather tell us what the children have in mind," Mrs. Meredith suggested.

"Thank you. They believe that if we can see that we are not separate we will serve all out of love. Basically, they believe that we no longer need systems in our schools that are based on separateness."

"This sounds New Age to me, and I don't appreciate it," Mr. Thorp said with authority. "I don't mean to be uncooperative, but the fact that our students are thinking like this and wanting to bring these crazy ideas into our schools scares me. I've heard people talking like this on some talk shows, and I know there are books written about these thoughts. Was this leadership conference sponsored by the schools and paid for with our tax dollars? If so, the board needs to talk about this. We wouldn't allow our children to be experimenting with drugs at a school function, and I don't think we should be very pleased about our kids experimenting with this kind of New Age thinking about how we are all one and connected by love and wanting this kind of thinking to change things in Winterhaven." Heather noticed a few heads nodding when Mr. Thorp finished his statement.

Just as things were beginning to get a little out of control, Mrs. Meredith said, "I think we're getting a little ahead of things. We're jumping to conclusions. I think we need to relax a bit and listen to Dr. Hosford. So far, all I've heard is that our student leaders are doing what I think all of us desire, and that is to see each other as a very unique person, and to not judge one another, and realize that we're all people with a common characteristic and that is being human. Having realized this, all they want to do is work together to meet children's needs rather than constantly separating people for one reason or another. So far, everything I've heard makes all the sense in the world, has no threat to church and state and is more common sense than New Age, whatever New Age really means." When Mrs. Meredith had finished, there was a feeling that she had made a good point, and it was back in Heather's hands. She thought she was saved by Myra and she would have to express her heartfelt appreciation for her words.

"Thank you, Mrs. Meredith, for putting my remarks in perspective. Let me go on and try to set the stage for what's to come. The students believe that we don't need special education as we have come to know it. They don't mean that we don't need to meet the educational needs of our children. Quite the contrary. They believe that we can meet the needs of students far better by unification than we can with separate systems.

"I'd ask each of you to listen with open minds when the school year begins. I think the children have a good idea, and I have pledged my support to them. It would be normal for each of us to be concerned that the children will attempt to change how we do business in Winterhaven. I have been there in my thinking, but I've learned from them, and I'm taking a risk with them, and with you. Please listen to them.

"I've invited Barbara, Emily, Brad, and Randy to join us this morning so you can begin today to hear their message. I ask you to welcome them and to listen to their words." With this brief introduction, the four students came into the board room. Ted, Sue, and Kathy were with them and sat quietly off to the side.

Dr. Hosford introduced each, and after a short silence, Barbara began, "Good morning. My friends and I are happy to be with you. We're thankful for Dr. Hosford's support and understanding. We're fortunate to have her leadership in our school district. Each of us would like to share some thoughts with you and then you may have some questions to ask. Emily will be first, followed by Brad and Randy, then I will be last. Emily?"

Unity and the Children

"We've come to realize that each of us is connected, and while our senses tell us that we are different, we are not. We are all one, and, being one, we love all. In loving all, we no longer judge, and not judging, we don't experience separateness. In our school, we see separateness yet we believe we are all connected."

Brad followed, "While you give those of us with disabilities a special experience, it's not special. In giving your special attention, you separate us and treat us differently because you see us or judge us as being different. Now, we have come to believe that being connected, we have no need to be treated as if we're different."

Randy began to push his computer keys. In a matter of seconds the words, "I WANT TO BE INCLUDED BECAUSE I AM CONNECTED," appeared on the screen. Not only were the adults present impressed with the technology, but the students as well as Ted, Kathy, and Sue were astounded at the length of his message. Heretofore, they had only seen a word or two.

Barbara then spoke, "As you begin to listen to us, I think I can summarize our thinking and the change we desire for Winterhaven by saying that we believe that if a procedure, practice, or system is good for any of us, it is good for all of us. For example, we label some children in Winterhaven. In special education, we label children by a characteristic. We say autistic, or learning disabled, or mentally impaired. We label children as gifted. When we label one, we label all of us as Emily implied. We would respond, that if labeling is not helpful for one of us, it is not helpful for any of us. Therefore, we will no longer label because to label one of us is to separate us."

Barbara continued, "Children up to now who are eligible for special education have a meeting designed to outline a plan that is designed so they have services and programs that meet their learning needs. If this is good for one of us, it is good for all of us.

We believe that individualized planning is good for one, and we would hope that all students in Winterhaven would have a meeting once a year to plan an appropriate program to meet individual needs.

"One more example: we can no longer accept the system we call special education. It is a separatist system. It applies only to certain students and it separates by labels, forms, meetings, teacher credentials, and dollars. Because it's based on separateness, it's not acceptable because our thinking is based on connectedness.

"I imagine you are thinking that we believe in no longer serving students who have learning problems. Nothing could be further from the truth. Because we're connected, we desire for each of us to learn, to be happy, to be growing in all areas of our development. But, we wouldn't do this by separating us. We do this by giving to another, because in doing this we give to ourselves since we are all one. We need teachers and therapists and service personnel because we need the knowledge and skill they possess. But we don't need separate classrooms, separate meetings, and separate forms. I repeat, if a process or procedure is deemed to be good for one, it is good for all. In our way of thinking, it is good for anyone to go to a human resource center for individual help. It's good for anyone who needs it to spend time with a speech and language therapist. It's good for any of us to talk to our social worker or psychologist if we or one of our teachers believe we can benefit from the experience.

"You see, it's our hope that you'll begin to see the transformation we think we need. The transformation we speak of will not be disruptive. We believe that a change in thinking will lead to a change in action, but the change need not be costly or disruptive in classrooms or in our schools. Finally, we ask you to think with us and to work with us to make the Winterhaven School System one that is based on unification and not separation. We're always available to each of you to answer questions or to meet with your members. Thank you."

When Barbara finished, there was a quiet, a kind of stillness and peace. People seemed to sit quietly and think about what she had said. Finally, Dr. Hosford broke the silence, "Thank you students for joining us. I have a feeling that much good will come from your work. Does anyone have a question?"

"Going too fast with this idea," Clark Ludlow said. "I think the theory of unification is good but there are so many factors to consider. I think we're about a year or two away from having a change of this magnitude take place, and that's only if the majority of the citizens and employees agree.

"I don't mean to be negative," Mr. Thorp added. "I think I'm a realist, and the reality of this is not going to work. We all know how hard it is to change anything, let alone a change the magnitude of what I think it is we're talking about. I mean, can you imagine the teachers responding to this? The union will want to know how this conflicts with their contract. They just won't buy it. The PTO will want to discuss and debate this. I mean, can you imagine a system without special education classes in Winterhaven? Let's get real here. The school board, as well-meaning as they are, are politicians who have trouble making a decision if citizens object to anything out of the ordinary. Finally, call it what you will, but when people hear about love, connectedness, unification, spirit, you'll have the board room packed with a lot of concerned people. This is right up there with suggesting that children just have a quiet moment to themselves. Don't get me wrong. I like the good thoughts and in another era or lifetime, this might have a chance, but let's get our heads out of the sand and face the realities here."

Barbara lowered her head as if in prayer. It was very quiet in the room. She lifted her head and said, "Everything Mr. Thorp has said is why the change must come from the children. The adults see everything through their conditioned experiences and their carefully constructed paradigms. When you view reality through separateness, you see conflict, difficulty, strain. When you see connectedness, you see unity and love. We haven't developed these strong patterns of what is, and, therefore, a lot of awakening or unlearning need not occur. We know that if they view connectedness, what they'll model and expect will be far different from what the adults impose on them from their perceptions of what should be."

Barbara continued, "The change for Winterhaven will come through the children and not through the school board or the PTO, or the union, or the superintendent's office, or a memo from the principals. The change is inside of us, it is not from the outside. You can look and look in the physical world of the senses and it will elude you. It's in you, in your hearts, your minds, your soul. Don't believe your eyes, for you are a victim of illusions. Believe with your heart and soul, and you'll come to see that we're all one, we're connected, and being connected, we love others because we are the others and the others are us. There's no separation. Knowing this, we, cannot accept an educational environment that reinforces separate systems. It's really quite simple, if you can view it from within instead of looking out into the world."

Randy had been putting a message into his computer and it read, "BELIEVE AND THE TRUTH WILL SET YOU FREE."

"Precisely, Randy," Emily said. "The truth sets us free when we realize that not knowing the truth imprisons us. It's as if a cell is surrounding our minds, limiting our limitless beings. The truth that love is all there is, and that love is what connects us all in unity is what sets us free, and being free, we know that we are limitless beings. Knowing that we are limitless means that anything is possible including changing our school system.

Barbara continued where Emily left off. "Once you change your attitude and cease being limitless, living for self, thinking that we are separate, and judging others, you too will be free. You'll know that we are all one, and you'll act on that vision and unification. As Brad said, it will occur naturally. The less you do, the more it will manifest. What's natural is effortless. Look at nature for this lesson. You don't see a great deal of work or a planning committee being formed for the sun to shine, for plants to grow, for sunsets to bring you great awe. Likewise, we needn't work when we allow what is truth to touch our souls."

Dr. Hosford suggested a stretch break. She could tell that the children were making an impact already. There were still skeptical people in the room. But there was no rebellion, no irrational challenges. People were undoubtedly uncomfortable with some of what they heard, but they couldn't deny that what they heard tugged at their hearts.

During the break, Dr. Hosford glanced at the clock on the wall in the back of the room. She saw Unity standing by the door. Heather smiled and Unity smiled back. Heather was beginning to see Unity in the words of the students and she knew that they had been transformed by the love of her spirit. She had a feeling in the peace of the moment that all was going to be fine. The challenges would be met with love, and in that way, they could not fail, because failure is the result of fear, and fear is the opposite of love, which is all that exists. So, lacking fear is to deny failure, and living in love is to be connected to all life.

Following the break there was continued discussion with a general agreement that the children may have some good ideas that would merit further discussion. The students were thanked for their ideas and for coming to the meeting. Each present offered a spirit of cooperation and a willingness to think about a unified school district, and to try to have an open mind about change. In turn, the children thanked everyone for the opportunity to share their thinking.

Chapter Fourteen

At one of the weekly meetings of the children, there was a very important discussion that centered around taking another look at how they would begin their work with the other children in each of their schools. They knew that seeds needed to be planted for a transformation of thinking among the students.

"School will open in a couple of weeks and we need to once again think about what we will do when school begins," Barbara said. "We talked about this at the sanctuary. Any ideas?"

Each silently thought for a moment and then Brad spoke, "Of course it would be easy if Unity would volunteer to give an assembly at each of our schools. That would be instant awareness and there would be nothing left to do." Each smiled and agreed that this would be great, but also each knew that while Unity would be with them and all the children, such a suggestion was unrealistic, and not the way in which change was to come to Winterhaven.

"I think our plan should involve the student councils," Emily suggested. "I also think we need to have an assembly as Brad suggested, where we talk with the students and explain our thinking."

Randy was putting words together in his computer. The others looked on his screen and saw, "PRESENT THE PLAN."

"Yes. Good idea, Randy," Barbara said with emotion. "We need to come forward with the unification plan when we provide our thinking. All people find change easier when they have something concrete to look at and consider. So, as Randy said, we should also present what we envision in our schools."

"Are we suggesting that our first presentation would be to our student councils and then to the student body as a whole?" Emily asked.

"That seems to make sense to me," Barbara said. "Do we agree?" Each nodded.

"Let's make sure we fully understand what the unification system looks like," Emily suggested.

"It must come from our belief statement and our set of principles," Brad offered. They put these in front of them on the table and continued their discussion.

Randy typed in, "NO LABELS."

"Yes, I agree," Barbara replied. "When we label another, we label ourselves. So, from the beginning we will propose the elimination of all words in our vocabularies that perpetuate differences and therefore separation. Many will say we are denying the reality of our physical, emotional, and intellectual characteristics. As we know, our reality is that we are all one. We realize that each of us has unique characteristics, but the words we have used are ones that contribute to judgment, separation and don't lead to unity."

Unity and the Children

Brad was next to speak. "Secondly, unification doesn't allow for the separation of students. So, there will be no classrooms provided for groups of labeled people. There will be learning centers available to all where individualized instruction or opportunities can be enjoyed.

"Third, we, the students, will take more responsibility for helping each other," Emily said. "With help from teachers who have knowledge and skill in individualizing instruction, we can provide instruction to each other."

"Fourth, we'll use our belief that if something is good for one, it's good for everyone," Barbara continued. "On the other hand, if something isn't good for all of us, it's not good for any of us. For example, if a comprehensive evaluation is a good thing for Brad, then each of us shall have one. If an individualized education plan is good for Randy, then each of us shall have one. If a plan to transition to the community is good for one of us, each of us shall have one."

"Fifth, we need to take responsibility, and to become self advocates for having our needs met. I can conduct my own meeting for individual planning," Brad added.

"Sixth, Dr. Hosford is concerned about the impact of the unification of Winterhaven on state and federal laws," Barbara reminded the group. "There is a future lawyers organization in the high school. I think about eight to ten students gather once a month to discuss their future profession. I think they'd be willing to take on a project of looking carefully at these laws and giving some suggestions on what needs to be done to meet the law, but still have unification.

"Finally, Dr. Hosford is concerned that our plan may limit dollars coming to the school district to support the services we all need, each student council has a treasurer. I suggest that a committee be set up involving the treasurers who would meet with the school's business administrator to look into this. I know that it's a very complicated system, but I'm sure that their collective thinking will yield some food for thought."

Ted added, "So far, what you've been discussing tends to fit into a mold of how we would devise the unification if we were starting from scratch, but some thought and planning needs to occur for the reality that in a couple of weeks a system will be in place. Children with disabilities have an individualized education plan agreed upon, which is like a contract, and it specifically says that they will be in a labeled classroom for a certain period of time with a special education teacher."

Ted continued, "The consolidated school district has a plan approved by the State Board of Education so dollars can flow here. The plan specifically shows that certain categorical classrooms will be in place. We have to count how many eligible students we have in Winterhaven, so that the district gets federal dollars. So, I hear you talking about how you would have a school system if one were to be created. But, if the transformation is to occur, there has to be a breaking apart of the current model, so to speak, so that the new way of thinking can prevail."

"Thanks, Mr. Traylor. He's right," Barbara admitted. "Do we hope for a total transformation on the first day of school, do we want a phase in, or do we just want a year of planning, thinking, and adjusting to a future change? I think we need Unity on this one. Let's just be silent for a few moments and ask for some guidance."

They all took her advice. After about five minutes, Unity was present in the room with them. She greeted each and the room was filled with light and peace. "All that you're doing is good. All of your thinking is leading to the transformation."

Unity and the Children

"We are needing to move from the theory stage to the implementation stage," Barbara remarked. "It's one thing to change a personal attitude or thought, but it is quite another to change a system. We decided we needed your wisdom once again."

They all sat quietly and in anticipation of what Unity would say. She began, "The change will come from you. Keep this uppermost in your minds. Change doesn't often come from the children. It comes from adults who write books and give motivational speeches, from boards of education, from superintendents, from principals, from teachers, and from politicians. Remember always that the change will come from you.

"This change is coming from the transformation of your minds. It is coming because you see a connectedness; you are standing up to your senses telling your brain that you see differences and then you allow judgment which separates. This separation leads to all kinds of frustration, division, and mistreatment of all. The task at hand, and the only task, is the transformation of thought from believing that each person is separated from all others to believing that we are all one. Just as you have gone through that and seen a unification as the result of your transformed thought, others will do the same. What is natural will flow from the transformed thought and an acceptance of truth. Once the people of Winterhaven see the truth, what follows has to be unification. It is the natural extension of the thought."

"How do we transform people's thinking?" Emily asked.

"You already have. Dr. Hosford is with you. Mr. Traylor, Mrs. Hickok, and Mrs. Wilson are thinking differently. The people in the meeting respected your thoughts. They are thinking differently."

"Yes, but you met with Mr. Traylor and Dr. Hosford. Can't you just meet with all the others and transform their thinking? It would be much easier and faster," Emily said.

"I'm meeting in my own way with everyone, Emily. I'm expecting that the process of change will take a long time, but it needs to begin. You will lead people through change, and the foundation will be in place for years to come.

"It is also time to prepare you for the fruits of your labors. Because of all that will happen in Winterhaven, you'll be asked to share, and your thoughts will go to others. You'll be traveling and talking to many. Your gift, the purpose of your existence, is to share your wisdom and to work toward the unification of all. Whenever you encounter frustration or fear, think back to this gathering and reconnect with truth, with love, with purpose and know that you cannot fail or fall into fear, for I am always with you." With that, Unity disappeared from the group and, as in the past, there remained a sense of intense calm and joy.

The people present felt refreshed, and once again they had a sense of direction. Barbara summarized, "It seems that the task at hand is the transformation of thinking from separation to unity and it also seems that what we have been doing is working. We need to continue to meet and share with people, believing that Unity is with us in our thinking, and in our action."

Chapter Fifteen

"I have a suggestion," Brad said.

"You often have good ideas, Brad. Please share it," Emily said.

"I think we should begin by having a before school picnic. Let's invite the principals from each of our schools as well as a special education teacher and a regular education teacher. We would also invite some parents, a student leader in the special education class and in the general education class."

"Yes, and I would add Mr. Thorp of the PTO, Mrs. Meredith of the school board, and finally, Dr. Hosford," Ted suggested. "If we can get some support from a few key leaders in the district, I think it just might catch on in other classes, and in other schools."

"Does everyone agree with the picnic idea and the people to invite?" Barbara asked. They all nodded in agreement. Randy got everyone's attention with another message on his computer, "SEPARATE MEETINGS FIRST."

"You think it would be better for us to meet with just the teachers, parents, or principals et cetera before a group meeting?" Barbara asked, addressing her question to Randy. Randy seemed to think for a moment and typed, "SMALL GROUPS." All seemed to agree with Randy's wisdom.

Mr. Traylor volunteered to set up the meetings with the teachers whom the students thought would be good initial leaders. Brad said his mother would be helpful in pulling together a meeting of parents of children with disabilities. Dr. Hosford would be asked to bring the principals together. The children would meet with the student leaders in the identified classrooms. It was agreed that all four meetings would be held the same day and evening. It would be a long day, but the day would be intense with much discussion and energy given to the fulfillment of the desire to unify Winterhaven. The day chosen was a Friday in mid-August. Arrangements were made, and to everyone's surprise most were eager to meet and to discuss the student's thinking.

———

The easiest meeting was with the students in the chosen classrooms. They thought the ideas were great. They couldn't understand the separation in the first place so asking them to welcome this new thinking and acting was like suggesting that common sense be the order of the day. They had one suggestion that seemed acceptable to all, and that was to create a system entitled SUPPORT which was an acronym for Students Upholding Partners by Planning, Orienting, Respecting, and Teaching. They believed that when people are connected, they would uphold one another because they would be upholding themselves. Further, they would see themselves as partners who would be interested and involved in planning, orienting or guiding, respecting the other and serving as a teacher in many ways. So, collectively yet as one, they determined that the SUPPORT program would be an integral component in the success of their transformation.

The special education teachers were skeptical of releasing control of the students with disabilities over to general education teachers. They were afraid that a few teachers may lose their jobs, and that the special education students would fail to get the attention they deserved. Finally, they were not sure they liked having non-disabled children come to their classrooms because it would mean more children to work with and would take away from their work with the disabled children. The cooperative teaching sounded like a challenge, but they felt that they would be treated like visitors in the general education classroom rather than accepted as an equal partner in educating all of the children.

The general education teachers were most fearful that they would not know what to do to help the disabled students. They thought they were already taking too much time and shortchanging the non-disabled children in their classes. They were not keen on sharing their classroom with another teacher or teachers. Call it turf if you will, but there is something about having a territory that is yours. They were not very happy about having an individualized plan for every student in their class as they already resented the time it took to attend the planning meetings for the students with disabilities in their classrooms.

For both sets of teachers, there was a certain challenge to the idea that did strike a chord of enthusiasm. After meeting with the students, they agreed to try it as long as everyone understood that it was only for a few months. This would allow time to see what problems surfaced. Both sets of teachers did ask that an evaluation plan be devised so that some objective data could be collected to serve as a focus for discussion after a few months of experimenting.

One refreshing aspect of the meeting was that the teachers agreed to try this plan without any mention of the union or needing to see anything in writing. They seemed to be doing it for the children of Winterhaven. There was an element of trust. When their meeting was concluded, it was agreed that: no labels would be used for students, teachers, or classrooms; an individualized education plan would be developed for each student in the classes, and each student's plan would be written at a parent-teacher conference; teachers would work together in planning, teaching, and evaluating; and, the special education class would now be called a Resource Center. Anyone could go there for individualized help, small group instruction, or for any reason as long as there was some type of adult supervision available. All students would follow the core curriculum unless a supplemental set of experiences or learner outcomes would be devised, and agreed upon by the teachers and parents.

—————

The principals' meeting went quite well. Their main concern was the reaction from the teachers and the parents. If it met with satisfaction from these two groups, then the principals were all for it. They also expressed concern about compliance with state and federal law, since monitors were scheduled to come to Winterhaven this year. The principals wanted it made clear that, if there were any problems coming from this plan, they wanted the school board to know that this new way of doing things was an agreed upon process so that no undue criticism would be forthcoming. This group of leaders had no objections. The plan seemed to make sense. They were in the middle with Dr. Hosford being favorable to the idea and if the parents and teachers found favor with it, then implementing it would be fairly routine.

—•—

The group that raised the most objections were the parents of both sets of children. The parents of the special education students were most skeptical. They thought this was a plan by the school board to limit services to their children. They had fought long and hard over the years to create the opportunities that were currently in place. If their children were placed back in regular education classrooms, something would have to be different because it was in this setting that failure was experienced, or if not failure, at least much frustration. The parents believed that the children would be shortchanged as the general education teacher would not have time for their children and the special education teacher would be working with all children, and not able to give their students the individualized attention they had come to appreciate.

The parents of the non-disabled children were also not sure this was a good idea. There is so much attention on high standards and needing to learn so much so fast so that scores on the state's assessment program would be favorable to the school board and to the citizens of Winterhaven. If the disabled students were in the general education classrooms, then all of the children may be held back and the lessons and curriculum would be, for lack of a better phrase, watered down. It wasn't that the parents objected to having children with disabilities in the same classroom as their non-disabled children; it was a matter of thinking that their children would get less quality teaching if such a plan were to be implemented.

After the meeting with Barbara, Emily, Brad, and Randy, it

was agreed, but not unanimously, that a pilot program could be tried. The parents thought it would be a good idea to meet once every two weeks during the pilot program to discuss concerns and to speak out if their fears were being realized.

———

At the end of the day of meetings, the children conducted a debriefing meeting with Dr. Hosford. They all concluded that the meetings went well. There was a spirit of willingness to give it a try. To a person, they thought Randy's idea of holding group meetings was a good one, since each group felt free to express its unique concerns.

It seemed obvious that people attending the meetings had not undergone any change in their thinking as the children had done. The transformation had not occurred and this, according to Unity, would have to happen for natural change to be forthcoming. Everyone seemed to give the idea a chance since the children were so enthused about it, and since Dr. Hosford was supportive. The students knew, though, that the transformation of thought would need to occur so that the change would take root and lead to a lasting change.

"Let's have the picnic now to celebrate getting off to a good start." Emily said.

"Absolutely. We'll have it in the city park where I met Unity for the first time. That would be kind of exciting, to get a new plan underway in the very spot where Unity helped me think differently," Heather said with a smile. "Before the picnic, I will have a talk with the school board president and the president of the PTO. This rounds out the people who need to be accepting of doing things differently if we are to get off to a good start when the school doors open in a couple of weeks."

Unity and the Children

Heather called Mr. Thorp of the PTO, and Mrs. Meredith, president of the Winterhaven School Board. They agreed to meet with her for dinner at a local restaurant. When they had completed their salads, Heather began the discussion, "I've asked you both here to continue the discussion of plans to follow the thinking of our student leaders.

"We would like to start in a few pilot classes in our elementary, middle, and high school. I suspect that we'll return some of our students from Timber Ridge. The teachers have asked for an evaluation component of the program. The parents were most skeptical but have agreed to try it for awhile. In my opinion, this will be the greatest thing we've ever attempted in Winterhaven. I say this because it comes from our children. Both of you know how hard it is to institute change when it comes from adults. However, this idea came from our students, and quite frankly it makes so much sense that people find it hard to criticize," Heather said.

"Will you be looking for approval from both of our groups?" Mr. Thorp asked.

"Yes. The students will be asking permission to address the school board at your next meeting, Mrs. Meredith, and they will want to address either the entire PTO or just your executive committee, Mr. Thorp."

"I think I'll take your lead, Heather. We hired you to guide this school district and to date you have done a fine job. I don't wish to start misjudging your decisions. I do think you are taking quite a risk with this, but I trust your judgment," Mrs. Meredith said, issuing a vote of confidence.

"I agree," Mr. Thorp said. "We've always subscribed to the theory that policy should be developed by the people who will be impacted by the policy, and by those who have to implement it.

So, if you, our principals, teachers, parents and students think it good policy, then who am I to get in the way. But, I do have a caution and I think it an important one. There are parents who are still not understanding this lady, Unity, and if this program gets too close to religion or to spirituality, I think you and Mrs. Meredith are going to have your hands full. There's not a lot of room for error on this matter. As you know, people are easily irritated when anyone tries to bring the secular and religious worlds together."

"Thanks, Mr. Thorp. We're going to have a real challenge there. I say this because you can't have a change based on people being connected without asking what connects us all. Once you believe that we are all connected, and it's pretty obvious that we aren't connected by anything physical, at least that is what our senses tell us. Therefore, we are connected by an unseen force, and could it be that this force is love. Once you agree that there is a connectedness in place, then what follows is that we can't judge another because we are only judging ourselves. An opposite effect becomes evident, and that is that we want what's best for another because we want what's best for ourselves. The next step is to believe that if we work together we can create a school system or community where people love each other. From that love comes compassion and a fair treatment of all. All of this sounds very spiritual to me, and even quite religious, if one were to take the words of great spiritual leaders of any worldwide religion. So, I understand your caution, but we'll just have to see what develops," Heather replied.

"Where do we go from here? Do you have permission from the state department or the federal office?" Mrs. Meredith asked.

"The government won't understand what we are doing or even if a few people do, they won't be able to endorse our plan, because they work from a system of separation. The children and

Unity and the Children

Unity have come to fulfill the law, meaning that when you act from connectedness and love you won't need any law. A law is only to control people. When left to act on their own, they respond to their separateness, their judgment, their discrimination and then they need to protect themselves from themselves. So, they pass laws to control what would occur naturally if people were looking at themselves as connected. The children are looking differently, and, therefore don't need any laws to have love flow and to act naturally.

"Back to your question, I'll talk with the state director and see if there can be any support for creativity or any flexibility to try something different. If I don't get any support from the government, I expect to take the ultimate risk and proceed. I'll take whatever sanctions might be forthcoming. My prediction is that what Winterhaven is creating will be the beginning of a new way of serving all children. There will be no one who will have the courage to challenge the common sense, and the results of our new way of thinking. If the school board has to fire me for what we do, I would leave with incredible pride, and I'd be thinking as I drove out of town, 'what a cause to give a career for!'"

"Let's give it a try. That's what I say," Mr. Thorp said with surprising enthusiasm.

"The students are planning a picnic this weekend and they plan to invite all who will be participating in their SUPPORT program when school opens. They'd be honored if the two of you would be able to attend. Can you make it?" Heather asked.

"You can count on me and thanks for your leadership, Heather. I get a feeling of calm talking with you," Myra said. "You have a spirit that communicates compassion for children. You have our full support. We wish you the very best."

Richard L. Baldwin

Chapter Sixteen

The day was perfect for a picnic. It was warm, the sky was blue, the grass was green, and a slight breeze touched all who were there on this festive day. People were arriving with their contribution to the potluck party. The sharing of food and the love that went into its preparation was an example of the unity that was to come.

Barbara and the other children were busy greeting and welcoming everyone to the picnic. Each car coming into the parking lot represented a spirit that would make a difference in the transformation of a school system. When all had gathered, and the table was full of the picnic food, Barbara said, "Thank you all for coming to our first get-together. Before we share our meal, I would ask that we form a circle. Would you do that for us?"

Immediately, all present stood around in a big circle, and

Barbara then said, "I would ask that we all join hands in our big circle and then I would ask that we all close our eyes. In this moment we are connected physically, but I would ask you to expand your thinking to believe that we are also connected in spirit. We are at this moment, and for all moments to come, one. As we go into the school year and face the challenges before us, may we reflect upon this moment, this moment when we ceased to see with our eyes and began to see with our hearts and souls."

While people were still in the circle, Emily asked each to reach out to others whom they did not know and make each other feel comfortable.

Brad then shared the planned events of the afternoon. After the shared meal, there would be recreation, which purpose was to play and be joyful and not to win or to conquer another. He smiled when he said that the picnic would end with his favorite picnic treat, S'mores: a toasted marshmallow between two squares of graham crackers and four squares of a Hershey chocolate bar.

Randy got everyone's attention. Dr. Hosford told all what Randy had typed into his computer, "LET'S EAT!" Everyone clapped their hands and the lines formed on both sides of the large picnic table. When all had received their helping and were seated on lawn chairs or at picnic tables, one of the teachers, who had not met or even heard of Unity, noticed a woman who did not appear to be with their group gathering some food from the table. She rose and approached her, "Can I help you?"

"I am where I am to be. I am here so that you will discover your purpose."

"My purpose. What do you mean?"

"The responsibility of teaching children is enormous. Your purpose is to realize their fragile existence and to help them understand that they are all connected. Being connected, they must have the opportunity to share their compassion with another, to love each other." As quickly as she had appeared, she was gone.

The teacher wondered what had just happened. She was talking to a woman at the picnic, was she not? She went back to her table and asked others, "Did you see me talking with a woman over by the food table?"

"Yes, we did. Is she with our group or did she just wander into our party?" a parent asked.

"I don't know. I was talking with her and she seemed kind of strange yet she was very loving and peaceful. She was talking about teaching and our enormous responsibility to support and love each other. Her words were strange but were said in such a beautiful way."

"Did you see her leave?" the teacher asked.

"No, we were talking about our plans for Labor Day."

The teacher didn't feel like eating. She felt as if she had just encountered love. She just wanted to bask in that feeling for a few moments.

When the meal was finished, and all had time to play some games, and once the S'mores were consumed much to the pleasure of all, Dr. Hosford got everyone's attention and said, "Today we begin a challenging journey envisioned by Barbara, Emily, Brad, and Randy. They will lead us to a compassionate school where our hearts and souls will guide where our eyes and other senses have previously ruled. Each of you are to be commended for taking a risk. I know that change is very difficult for people and quite frankly it scares me a little, too. But I've never been as confident about a positive change as I am today. I've a sense that next year's picnic, and I hereby declare this to be an annual get-together to celebrate our connectedness and our vision for a unified Winterhaven School District, will be a celebration of joy. I am very hopeful that as people in Winterhaven, and the visitors we no doubt will entertain from throughout our state and country will say when they leave, that they knew us by our love; our love of teaching, our love of children, our love of supporting each other, and our love of one another. We shall never forget this day of unity."

⎯⎯⸱⸱⎯⎯

As planned, Barbara, Brad, Emily, and Randy spoke before the school board on the Tuesday evening following the picnic. With Mrs. Meredith's support and after several thought-provoking questions and excellent answers, the school board offered support for the pilot program. The board asked that Dr. Hosford write a report outlining the legal and fiscal problems that may be encountered in implementing the plan. She agreed to report in a matter of weeks.

Likewise, the children met with the executive committee of the PTO. Just as Mrs. Meredith offered support before the school board, Mr. Thorp was most enthusiastic in his endorsement of the plan. He assured the committee that parents and teachers of special and general education students were involved in the plan and all seemed to support the concept, at least for the purpose of having a few pilot classes in Winterhaven. As with the school board, after a round of good questions and confident answers by Barbara, Emily, Brad, and Randy, the executive committee gave unanimous endorsement of the plan. They asked for a presentation in a few months so they could discuss the merits of the student's ideas and to discuss any problems that seemed evident at that time.

The stage had been set. A lot had happened since the students crafted their plan at the Wildlife Sanctuary in the early summer. They had gotten the support from all parts of the school community in Winterhaven. They had a unity picnic, and presented themselves well before the school board and the PTO. The foundation was in place, the groundwork had been completed. All was ready for school to open in a few days.

Chapter Seventeen

Dr. Hosford asked for a meeting of the parents of these student leaders. She wanted to meet with the students, too. But for a few minutes she wanted to talk with their parents. All were asked to come to her office for a meeting late in the afternoon. Barbara's mother, Valerie Conrad, was the first to arrive. She was the vice president for sales at a manufacturing plant between Winterhaven and Springday. In fact, she was the first African-American to fill a high level corporate position in the Winterhaven area. Heather was a believer in the theory that leaders are made and not born, but in this case Barbara just may have inherited some fine leadership qualities from her mother.

Randy's father, Bob Lubienski, arrived next and introduced Randy's stepmother, Linda, to Mrs. Conrad and to Dr. Hosford. Mr. Lubienski was the butcher at the local grocery store. He was quite popular with the shoppers because he made sure all the cooks in

Winterhaven got choice cuts for their special celebrations; birthdays, anniversaries, and weddings.

Brad's foster parents, Larry and Elizabeth Sommers, were the next to arrive and they were followed by Brad's grandmother, Marilyn Proudfoot, who couldn't raise him, but who took an intense interest in Brad's schooling. She was a Native American whose ancestors lived in the Winterhaven area before the arrival of the white people. Brad often gave much credit to his grandmother, telling people that she was his strength, his example of a loving person.

Emily's mother and father, Joe and Marie Hernandez, were the last to arrive. They apologized for being a bit late. Mrs. Hernandez said they were delayed at the travel agency; they needed to get their tickets to go to Mexico for a large family reunion.

When all had arrived and met each other, Dr. Hosford spoke, "I've asked you to come together for a couple of reasons. I know you are proud of Barbara, Brad, Emily, and Randy. I wanted to tell you in person that I, too, am very proud of them. They have worked together to help people see that we are all connected. They have collectively been responsible for this school district coming to the beginning of a transformation. So, thank you for being supportive parents and providing wonderful models for your children to emulate. My second reason for asking you to come together is to satisfy my curiosity. Did you know of the experiences your children were having in arriving at their transformed thinking?"

Barbara's mother, Valerie, spoke first. "It is very kind and thoughtful of you to say such wonderful things about our children. Barbara told me of her meeting Unity at her student council meeting last spring. She also told me of her experiences at the Wildlife Sanctuary, and this was not surprising to me at all.

"Unity has been in my life. When Barbara's father died several years ago, I was feeling such remorse that I felt like life was not worth living. Unity came to me and gave me wisdom and strength to carry on. When I finished talking with her, I felt a sense of peace, calm and love. Since that day, I knew I was a new woman and have lived a life of service to others because that was Unity's message to me. She said that by giving myself to others, I'd be giving energy to myself. I have come to realize that she was right. My ego would rather have me be selfish and serve all of my desires, but Unity's message was just the opposite; the more I give to others, the more love I receive. Please forgive me if I sound pious. I don't mean that. I'm telling you what I learned, and a natural flow of love comes to me when I serve others instead of myself. So, when Barbara said she had experiences with Unity, I knew my prayers were answered. I knew my daughter was safe and secure in the wisdom of her spirit."

Randy's father spoke next. "Like Valerie, I too have met Unity. I met Unity the day that Randy was born. His mother and I knew that Randy was not normal. We couldn't believe that we had a deformed child whom the doctor said would never walk or live a normal life. We were devastated. As we were together in the hospital room with Randy in his mother's arms, Unity appeared and talked with us. I can see her as if it happened a few minutes ago. She said, 'This son of yours is love. His soul, his spirit is just as pure as yours. Always know that the physical challenge that is his and yours is a gift, and an opportunity to fulfill a purpose. Your son and you are in my care now and forever. There is no fear. There is only love. Your son will grow up to unify people.' And, with that, she left us. My wife and I never felt such love before. We were immediately at peace. That feeling has never been as intense as it was that afternoon in the hospital room. So, when Randy would use his computer to communicate with me, I knew that Unity had fulfilled the statement made many years ago."

Brad's grandmother was next to speak. "I, too, thank you for your comments and I thank you on behalf of Brad's mother and father who are not here in the physical realm to say 'thank you,' but if you are quiet and listen, you will hear their voices. I'm also very thankful for Mr. and Mrs. Sommers who are giving him much love and support in his young years. Brad told me about meeting Unity last spring and talking with her at the leadership camp a couple of months ago.

"Like Valerie and Bob, I, too, have met Unity. I was a little girl growing up in Winterhaven many, many years ago. I was having a tough time dealing with being treated unfairly by people. Indians were not considered to be worthy citizens in town and there were many hurtful things said and done to us. As much as my parents tried to explain why we were being treated this way, I couldn't accept it. I was about twelve or thirteen. I was alone, taking a walk in the woods near our home when Unity appeared. She was beautiful and I felt so much love just being near her. She said, 'You are not your body or your mind. You are a loving spirit. The people who harm you with voice and action have momentarily forgotten who they are. They, too, are loving spirits, but they are asleep. Love them because you are one with them in spirit. This message you must hand down to your children and their children. I will be with you when you do this. She then disappeared as quickly as she had appeared. So, when Brad told me about Unity, I knew that she was fulfilling her love comment of many, many years ago. I can't tell you what joy is in my heart to know that Brad is living his life in a way that carries that message to others."

Finally, Marie Hernandez spoke. "Like the rest of you, we thank you, Dr. Hosford, for your kind words. We're very proud of Emily and are very pleased to know that she is using her intelligence and personality to help people. We are touched with your experiences of meeting, listening, and learning from Unity, but we have not met her. Emily told us of her experience meeting her in the cafetorium at the middle school, and of talking with her a few times since then. At first, I will admit that I was fearful that maybe Emily was experimenting with drugs which just couldn't be, but when she said she talked with a spirit on more than one occasion you can understand that we were concerned and hoped she wasn't holding our worst fears from us."

Mr. Hernandez interrupted, "Marie. Excuse me, but I must tell you and the others that I have met Unity. I just didn't say anything to you because I didn't think you would believe me. When I was in the war, I was very confused about all the killing I was witnessing and participating in. It was a most stressful time and Unity appeared and talked with me. Like Bob, I will never forget what she said. She held me and said, 'This is an illusion. This is not love because only love is real. Your soul and your spirit are free and living in a state of perfect love. This nightmare that you are experiencing is loveless, because all of the people are failing to see that they are connected. They see only separation and fear. Acting on fear, judgment, and separation they allow hate to cloud and to mask the real self, which is love. When you go within to seek the spirit in you, you will be bathed in love and peace. I am always with you, holding you, and am one with your spirit.' She left, and I just broke down and wept because I had never sensed such peace and calm.

"So, when Emily said that she had met a woman named Unity, I knew that she was having the same experience I had. I was so thankful it was not in something as terrible as war. I'm sorry, Marie, I just thought you wouldn't understand if I told you, but listening to these stories I realized I was not abnormal and felt I could, for the first time, tell you and others." Marie gave him a hug and others shared warm and loving thoughts.

Richard L. Baldwin

"I guess one thing we have in common is Unity," Heather said. "How fortunate we are to have met her and to have our lives enriched by her loving presence and guidance. This can't just be a phenomenon that a few people share."

"No, we are not any different than other souls," Barbara said. "We all seek love, and each in our own way meet Unity. Unity is within each of us. Unity is manifested in many ways so that each person or each soul has a unity experience once or many times in their lifetime."

Just then Unity appeared in the room. "It is time. It is time for unity to prevail and for the children and others in Winterhaven to understand their nature. My children, your hour is come. You shall lead others to the peace of mind that comes with accepting that love is the most powerful and most important attribute of a human being. I say this because it is the only way to have our unity be understood. Your sharing and your memories of me, warm my soul, and my love remains with you now and forever." She disappeared and all in the room were filled with peace and love.

Chapter Eighteen

The first day of school was much like the opening day of school for any year. Students, teachers, parents, and administrators met the day with mixed emotions. Most were eager for the routine to become established. Others were not wanting the vacation to end. It seemed like it had begun only a week or two ago.

The day before the students arrived, the staff of each school met with their principal in the afternoon. In the morning, Superintendent Hosford addressed the entire school staff. Those present heard her say, "This year will be an exciting year for Winterhaven. Our student leaders have designed a program for us to pilot. The concept is quite simple but the implications cause quite a transformation in our system. The thinking of some of our students is that we're all connected, and by recognizing this we cease to recognize separation. They, along with volunteer teachers in each of our schools, will begin a program that brings down the barriers of separation. So, for some children and classes in the pilot there will be no more labeling of children, no more separation of children because of their disabilities. Instead, teachers and students will work together to implement project SUPPORT, which is an acronym for Students Upholding Partners by Planning, Orienting, Respecting, and Teaching. I am sure you will be hearing more about this exciting program as the year progresses. I do want to add that I'm very proud of the students, their parents, their teachers, and others who are taking a risk in helping us change our attitudes about how we view ourselves, and how we act on these perceptions.

"For your information, this project is the outgrowth of the summer student leadership program which we sponsor at the Wildlife Sanctuary. The students who get the credit for this idea are Barbara Conrad of the high school, Emily Hernandez of our middle school, Brad Proudfoot of the elementary school, and Randy Lubienski of the Timber Ridge School. I'd like to bring them out and ask that you express your appreciation for their leadership with an enthusiastic round of applause." The four students came out onto the stage of the high school auditorium and acknowledged the warm round of applause given to them by the Winterhaven staff. Most in the audience didn't know what was about to happen, but the teachers and aides who were to give this a try did, and they were pleased to join in honoring the students. Never before had an idea of this significance come forth and at the root of it, was the children of Winterhaven.

After lunch, the staff met with their principal. Barbara, Emily, Brad, and Randy were available at each school for several minutes to answer any questions that might be asked by the staff. In general, people were pleased with the idea and proud of the students for their leadership. The principal of each school introduced the pilot teachers to their respective staffs. The teachers who would be involved commented about their plans, and the four students briefly explained project SUPPORT.

———•———

Dr. Hosford was at her home beginning to unwind from the first day of school when the phone rang. Whenever school was in session and the phone rang, it always caused a moment of anxiety because she was ready for anything. In all of her years of being a principal and superintendent she took calls informing her of: deaths of staff or their family members, school bus accidents, vandalism of school property, parents very upset with teachers, bus drivers or principals. It seemed that the sound of the phone ringing was synonymous with bad news or something that required her leadership. She knew that all of this came with the territory, but the reality of the phone ring bringing her a crisis could not be escaped.

"Hello."

"Dr. Hosford?"

"Yes."

"Dr. Hosford, this is Sally Quackenbush at the Daily News."

"Oh, hi, Sally. How're you?" Heather knew Sally and knew that she could trust her for fair and accurate reporting. She was a friend of the school district and had been very helpful in past millage campaigns.

"I'm fine, thanks. I know this was your first day of school. Is everything off to a good start?"

"Absolutely. I feel better about this opening than any in the past ten years or so. How can I help you, Sally?"

"We have gotten several calls from parents concerned that you are removing special education from Winterhaven."

"That's not true. I mean, it's true if one thinks of special education as labeling children, separating them in special rooms, requiring they be seen by a limited number of people who have specific credentials. The children are helping us to see the need to be unified instead of separate. But, on the other hand, children are getting all the attention they need, and I am convinced that when the pilots are complete and the evaluation report is finished, this school district will be enjoying positive change that benefits everyone."

"The callers are pretty upset. They want us to report this to the citizens, and to even get into investigative reporting concerning how this may be contrary to state and federal law. They say you and the board cannot act like this. They say that because the Winterhaven School District receives federal funds, you must adhere to state and federal law."

"We are!" Heather said, getting a bit upset. "Who's calling, Sally? Can you tell me?"

"The people are parents of students at the Timber Ridge School. They told me they'll be calling our state senator and representative. They said they will be at the next school board meeting to protest this threat to the long-established system that they worked so hard to get."

"I shouldn't admit this to you, but with all the planning we did this summer, I guess we did overlook that group. We didn't think our plan would bother them. The parents of children in Winterhaven were supportive because we indicated that they would have a choice of coming back to Winterhaven and participating in our pilot or remaining at Timber Ridge. I didn't think that this would cause a concern to the parents from other school districts."

"They see what you are doing as being the beginning of the end of their separate school, which they desperately want to continue for their children. They don't want to have to return their children to their communities for schooling. They say that once this happens in Winterhaven, it will spread to Summerville and Springday."

"We'll handle it somehow. What do you need from me?"

"Well, I've always been a real fan of Heather Hosford, you know that. I definitely don't want to cast you, your board, or the students who developed this idea in any bad light, but my newspaper training taught me to tell the truth, to communicate to my readers what is factual, and to do so in an objective way."

"That's why I have such a high regard for you, Sally."

"I guess I'd like to do an article about what you are doing in Winterhaven, include a quote or two from you, and perhaps Barbara Conrad and maybe Randy Lubienski. After all, he is a student at the Timber Ridge School, and his father is very supportive of your work, isn't he?"

"Yes."

"Why don't I do this. I'll develop a short story and include a few quotes from you and others. That should settle the demand to see the *Daily News* become involved. Then in a few weeks, I'll do a positive story about project SUPPORT, assuming there will be a positive story to report. You'll probably get a call from the legislators."

"Oh, I can't wait. I'll have them both in here to see our pilots and how working together can lead to quality programming for all. I remember my mother telling me over and over that a problem is only an opportunity in disguise. All that you've shared with me gives me a great chance to work with the children to confront the people living in darkness. Not to judge them, because I'm trying to learn that we are all connected and these parents are me. My challenge is before me and I thank you for alerting me to it, Sally. If I can ever help you, just let me know. We're not, as you know, supposed to develop relationships with the media, but I've always considered you a professional friend and I thank you for your call."

The next edition of the *Winterhaven Daily News* arrived on porches with the lead article in Section B being, "Children Lead Changes in Winterhaven Schools." Sally put forth the facts concerning the changes that were underway. There were four quotes in the article. The first was from Barbara Conrad, "Separation of students because of physical, emotional, or mental characteristics is an outmoded system of serving people. It takes the realization that we are all connected to know that separation supports labeling, separate classes, separate teachers, separate schools, separate laws, forms and dollars. The students of Winterhaven now have project SUPPORT, and we are living our connectedness."

Dr. Hosford was quoted as saying, "Change is very difficult for people to handle. The status quo clings to us and begs us to keep doing what we have always done. It is time to listen to our children and to realize that separate systems do not lead to the results we desire for all of Winterhaven's students."

The leader of the parent movement to challenge project SUPPORT and the new thinking offered by the children was Mr. Rayman. He was quoted this way: "Getting rid of special education is a big mistake. Children with disabilities have a right to special teachers, special classes, our special school, and to all the rights afforded our children by the Congress and our state legislators. This is a big mistake, and we will fight it with all the protections given us by law. We are angry about this and will be doing all we can to maintain our special education system."

The final quote was by Randy's father. "I understand the feelings of the parents who have children at Timber Ridge. I used to think like they're thinking and I don't judge them or condemn them. I'm just as connected to them as I am to my son and all the fine people in the Winterhaven School System. These parents have lived in anger and fear because of all the discrimination and ridicule they and their children have had to endure for years.

"They have learned that they can trust their separate system because it understands disability, it offers compassion from teachers, aides, administrators and the parents who share their good fortune in having a school like Timber Ridge. But, I believe the time has come in the evolution of education to unify the systems and to listen to our children and begin again. I ask my fellow parents of Timber Ridge to open their hearts, and to take the negative energy used to fight this and turn it into positive energy to trust the change, to support our children and teachers as they try to unify us."

The article had a picture of Barbara, Emily, Brad, and Randy as well as a classroom photo showing the teachers team teaching and the students working together.

Dr. Hosford had learned long ago that it is better to be on the offense than the defense. She called her representative, Mrs. Phillips who served the district where Winterhaven was located, as well as Senator Veldman. She spoke to their administrative assistants and invited each to visit Winterhaven Schools the next time they were in town. They were involved in an exciting transformation in the school district and wanted to keep them informed as she knew they would be proud of Project SUPPORT. The assistants said they would pass on the message to their respective legislators and thanked Dr. Hosford for calling.

Heather hung up the phone and called the director of special education in the state department as well as the Office of Civil Rights. She also called the United States Department of Education – Office of Special Education Programs. She told each that her school district was involved in some exciting efforts to reform education in Winterhaven. They were meeting the educational needs of all children eligible for special education under state and federal law. They were also adhering to all laws of the federal and state governments, but doing so in a different manner than has become traditional in the state and country. She invited each to visit and become a part of the exciting transformation of thinking. She was polite, firm, and respectful. She also learned early in her leadership career that offending anyone or causing them to go on the defensive gains nothing for her or anyone in her school district. Anger begets anger, and negativity spawns negativity. She learned to be upbeat, positive, and loving. This philosophy had gotten her much further over the years.

Barbara and Brad stopped by Dr. Hosford's office after school the day the newspaper article appeared. They asked Eleanor if they could see Dr. Hosford for a few minutes. She was on the phone, but would see the children shortly.

When they did meet, they discussed what they should do from this point forward. Barbara began, "Well, I guess we missed an important group in our briefings."

"Yes, I think so. No problem. This is only one of many little obstacles we'll face and deal with over the next several months. By the way, I called our senator and representative. I also called the state and federal directors of special education and the director of the office of civil rights. I think our briefings need to go a bit beyond Winterhaven," Heather said.

"Shall we set up a meeting with the parent group at Timber Ridge?" Brad asked.

"That might be a good idea. I'll call Mr. Brewer and talk to him about it.

"Sounds good to me," Barbara replied. "By the way, Emily, Brad, and I will be meeting with our student councils next week. We plan to discuss Project SUPPORT and put some time on the agenda at each meeting to talk about progress or lack of it. Any words of advice for us?"

"I don't think so. Each of you is doing a great job. I'm very confident of your work. Let me know following your initial meetings if all is going well. I will plan to add Project SUPPORT to the monthly principals' meeting agenda. Your discussion plus mine will keep your efforts on the minds of the students and staff.

"Oh, I almost forgot. Mr. Brewer called after the newspaper article appeared. He was sorry all of this is happening, meaning the reaction of his parent group. He should have predicted it, but really didn't think they would respond since the plan was for Winterhaven and no family was being urged to take its child from Timber Ridge and enroll him or her back in Winterhaven. I thanked him for his call. He's a good friend and leader. You watch, he will play a key part in the change at Timber Ridge."

The first day at Snow Castle Elementary School went smoothly. The special education teacher Miss Keyton worked well with the two general education teachers Mrs. Wethy and Mr. Harris who had volunteered for Project SUPPORT. Miss Keyton's special education classroom was introduced as being a center for anyone in the three classrooms who wanted to use it for a learning center. There would be a quiet place for independent work. There were many supplemental materials for all students to use.

Each child was given a form which was called My Individualized Plan or the MIP which was to be completed by the student. Each was to arrange a meeting with his or her parents and teacher. If they wanted the psychologist or social worker to be present, they would be invited. Each student was to write down his or her academic goals, and the group would construct a few objectives for the goals. The MIP would serve as a part of each student's portfolio, which would contain information about the student.

Also on the first day, each student was placed in a random group of four. They were to help each other and be peer tutors.

Part of each day was devoted to meeting as a group.

Miss Keyton arranged her day between supervising the Resource Center and team teaching in two general education classrooms. Mr. Harris and Mrs. Wethy thought it best initially for Miss Keyton to meet on a regular basis with the children who had reading difficulties. This took place early in the day while the other teachers were working on reading. She used a multisensory approach which was also a great help to other children who were not eligible for special assistance but who needed individual help using some of the traditional techniques of special education.

The first day in the high school went well too. This was Randy's first day in high school. He went to his homeroom in a new motorized chair accompanied by his computer. The students were quite accepting of him. Many were curious about his disability and the technology he used to communicate. He had a flag made of the school colors with the nickname of the school sewn on. This was quite a hit and helped him establish a degree of acceptance on the part of the students. It was Randy's way of expressing a connectedness with his peers.

Finally, the middle school too, accepted the initial phase of Project SUPPORT. Emily felt good about the first day. The only thing out of the ordinary was an incident on the radio. Toboggan Middle School has their own radio station which was the brainchild of the school's science teacher and a couple of students who enjoy electronics and technology. Each morning a few students make announcements and play a popular song of the day. The students are free to comment as they wish. So far, the freedom has been accompanied with responsibility which pleased the principal, Mrs. Worley. Everyone knew that the first time the privilege was misused the student radio station would, to use the vernacular, "Go off the air."

Unity and the Children

This morning one of the student announcers said, "Today is the beginning of a new school year and a new project at Toboggan Run. Today the sped classrooms cease to exist. We welcome the special education kids to our rooms and urge all Toboggan students to cooperate in making these kids feel welcome." There were a few snickers when he finished and many were embarrassed by his poor choice of words. Emily went right to the "radio station" and confronted the student, Mark Williams, who looked like he was getting a lecture from the faculty sponsor, Mr. Lincoln."

"What did I do wrong?"

"You said 'sped' and talked about these students as if they were visitors in our school. It was a very insensitive thing to say Mark, very inappropriate," Mr. Lincoln offered.

"We all say 'speds'. It just means they go to a special education room. No big deal. You ought to hear what kids call me and the guys I hang around with."

"You may be right. Kids do have words and phrases for groups of people, but that doesn't make it right. The reason for Project SUPPORT is to help us all understand that we are connected and not separate. What you said reinforces the separation."

"I'm sorry. I didn't mean to hurt anyone."

"I think if you put yourself in the shoes of a student with a disability you would feel hurt hearing what you said, especially saying it in front of the whole school."

"Guess I wouldn't like it."

"What do you think you can do to change this, Mark?" Emily asked.

As Mark thought for a minute, Emily said, "Mark meant no harm with what he said. I suggest that Mark be the official Project SUPPORT reporter for the radio station. That way he could really get involved in what we are trying to accomplish, and I think it would help him understand. We need someone to get on the radio from time to time and Mark would be a fine reporter for the project."

"How do you feel about that, Mark?" Mr. Lincoln asked.

"That'd be okay with me."

"I'm sure Emily can help you understand the project. How about a weekly presentation, written by and reported by Mark Williams," Mr. Lincoln proposed.

After Mark had left, Mr. Lincoln said to Emily, "You handled that beautifully. Thanks."

"Thanks for accepting my suggestion. I was just trying to make a problem an opportunity."

Chapter Nineteen

The first meeting of the school year for the Timber Ridge Parent Association was called to order by their president Mrs. Sterling. After introducing a few new parents, Mrs. Sterling reviewed the agenda for the meeting. The agenda was quite traditional with a review of the minutes of the previous meeting, the treasurer's report, old and new business. They were beginning to plan the holiday bazaar and the school holiday program, which was a tradition dating back to the opening of the school more than thirty years ago. In fact, some parents and former students return each year for this festive and memorable program. It is school policy that every student at Timber Ridge participate in the pageant.

Mr. Albeck stood and asked to be recognized. Mr. Albeck's daughter, Alicia, has been a student at Timber Ridge for almost twenty years. "Yes, Mr. Albeck. Do you have an item for the agenda?" Mrs. Sterling asked.

"I want to talk about the newspaper article and the changes going on in Winterhaven."

"Okay, let's put that under new business. Are there any other additions to the agenda? Hearing none, I move that our agenda be accepted as is with the addition of Mr. Albeck's request to discuss the Winterhaven program. All in favor?" Everyone said, "Aye."

"All opposed?" Silence. "The agenda is set."

The meeting progressed normally, and after a break, Mrs. Sterling came to that point in the agenda when they were to discuss Mr. Albeck's concern. "Mr. Albeck, would you like to introduce your item?"

"Yes, thank you. I am assuming all of you know what I am talking about. We heard that Winterhaven is listening to some kids who got some hair-brained idea to get rid of special education. I could see this coming from cost conscious administrators or some radical group, but the children! I mean, what do they know? Special education is as American as mom, apple pie, and Chevrolet. What is going on here?" Mr. Albeck said, obviously upset.

Mr. Brewer stood to address the group. "Let me try to explain. Each year the student leaders of Winterhaven go to the Wildlife Sanctuary for a week long leadership conference. They are divided into groups and each group is asked to develop a project. We are invited to send one of our student leaders and this year I asked Randy Lubienski if he would like to participate. He said he would, and his father was supportive of Randy going along. In fact, Randy's aide and nurse also accompanied him to the conference.

"The students think that we're all connected and being connected by an invisible force which, for lack of a better word, I'll call love, we no longer see each other as separate. Not seeing each person as separate causes people to believe that we should not participate in activities that separate people. A real example of this is special education where children have labels, separate classrooms, and in the case of Timber Ridge, a separate school. The children then created Project SUPPORT which stands for Students Upholding Partners by Planning, Orienting, Respecting and Teaching."

"That's ridiculous!" Mr. Ledinsky shouted. "How can a bunch of kids change what's good for us and our kids with disabilities?"

"Well, they shared their idea with Superintendent Hosford and they met with groups of teachers, parents, students, and principals. Most agreed with the concept and said they would give it a try."

"Give what a try? How can you give special instruction by special teachers to special kids without special education?" Mrs. Lafferty asked.

"For starters, they do not label the kids."

"Are they denying reality? I mean. Face it. My kid is retarded. It isn't a four letter word for crying out loud. Why not teach people to respect people who have disabilities instead of refusing to use words that describe what our kids are or have. They're in some type of utopia, if you ask me," Mrs. O'Brien said.

"Labels communicate separation..." Mr. Brewer tried to explain.

"So does the word 'man' and 'woman' communicate separation. Do they want to stop using any word that separates people? Give me a break," Mr. Albeck said agitating the group.

"The labels we use do describe very real characteristics that many of us have, but the labels also have connotations and many of the connotations are negative," Mr. Brewer explained. "They have given people the impression that people with disabilities are not able to do many things. So, the children are not denying that people have characteristics, but they do believe that we should not use words that assist people in judging, discriminating, and separating."

"Okay, so no labels. What else?" Mr. Ledinsky asked.

"They do not believe in separate classrooms for students with disabilities."

"Where do the disabled kids go then?"

"They remain in the general education classroom and the special education teacher comes to the general education class and helps all who need assistance."

"How do you get individualization and small group help in a big class with all kinds of kids? Where are these kids getting this?"

"The special education classroom has become the school resource center where any student can get some individualized assistance or where a small group of students can work on a project or get some small group instruction because they aren't understanding a concept, for example," Mr. Brewer explained, feeling the anger of those in the audience. He, however, felt confident and peaceful in explaining the unification plan to others.

"I suppose they threw out the IEP, too," Mrs. O'Brien said a bit sarcastically.

"No. Actually, every student in the school will have an individualized education plan. The children believe that if something is good for one, it is good for all. So, all students will have an individualized plan. All will have a transition plan, and all will have a portfolio that describes each student's putting forth his or her interests, skills, talents, test scores, letters of recommendation, attendance, et cetera."

"Do these students think we shouldn't have Timber Ridge?" shouted someone in the audience.

"You will have to ask them, but I can tell you that a separate school would not fit their thinking of unity and connectedness."

"If they think this place is going to close because some kids believe we are all connected, they need to get turned around in their thinking. I can't believe adults are falling for this stuff. Usually common sense prevails when crazy ideas come up, but where is common sense? Where is it? We are the common sense and we must speak up and stop this craziness," Mr. Baldus said with much emotion.

Just then the door opened and in walked Unity. She was with Barbara, Emily, Brad, and Randy. She and the children walked to the front of the room and there was a sense of peace and calm that had not been present during the evening. Unity lowered her head for a moment. Slowly she raised her head and began to talk. "Hello. My name is Unity. You're distressed and I feel your anger and your fear. There's nothing to fear for there is only love which conquers fear. Please listen to these students. They're the hope for our future. Please pay attention and open your hearts and minds to what they say. Their words are difficult for you because they speak from their soul and from the unity that is beyond what you can see and hear and touch and smell and taste. They speak from a connectedness that exists, which you can't sense with your physical bodies, but you can join the children and sense it with your hearts. Do not be anxious. Do not worry. Do not be angry. Live only for love, speak only of love, and above all, see that all of you are one. Being one, you cannot bring harm or judgment or anger or frustration to another because you will only bring it to yourself as you are doing tonight. It is time to follow the children. They are extensions of my spirit. I love you and am always with you." With that she was gone from the group and only the children were facing the parent group.

"The woman who just spoke is Unity and she has been the spirit of our thoughts and our actions," Barbara explained. "We bring a transformation of thinking that will unify Winterhaven and hopefully many more school districts. We are hoping that you, along with the teachers of Timber Ridge, and the students here will sense our connectedness, and will end the separation that has gone on for so many years."

"Timber Ridge has been here for you and your children in a time when separation was the only way to get an education, to get opportunities to learn and socialize," Emily remarked. "You found strength in coming together. Now is the time to see our connectedness and come together in a unified school system where our action is out of love for one another, and our unique characteristics are celebrated and not judged as being different."

"The two systems must come together," Brad said. "What has been good about special education needs to be in place for all children. What has not been good for all needs to stop. Everyone in the school should have individualized attention. Everyone needs to have access to specialists in learning styles, curriculums, and technology. The dollars should be pooled to serve all children. You see, separate laws and funding systems reinforce our separation. It's unity we seek for all."

Randy was busy feeding his computer. Barbara went over to him and read, "IT IS TIME TO CHANGE."

The room was quiet. It remained calm and loving as it was when Unity was present. There were no questions, no raised voices, no harsh comments. After a couple of minutes, Mrs. Sterling said, "I think Unity and the students have given us much to think about. I suggest we adjourn, interact with these children, and I'll be informing you of our next meeting. Thank you for coming. Thank you, Mr. Brewer, and thank you, students, for sharing your thoughts with us this evening."

The meeting was over. Some stayed to talk, but most quietly got up, put on jackets, and went silently to their cars. They didn't seem dejected or anything of the sort. They seemed to have been in the presence of intense love, and the only reaction to this peace and truth was to be struck with awe and wonder.

When Barbara got home she called Dr. Hosford. "Sorry to bother you, but I just wanted you to know that Unity and the four of us were at the Timber Ridge Parent Association meeting this evening. We were listening outside the door while Mr. Brewer was doing an excellent job of responding to the parents' questions. Just before we went in, Unity joined us and said that she thought we would need a little help with this group. We all went to the front. Unity offered some words and left. We then spoke and Randy finished by telling people that it is time for Timber Ridge to change. The meeting was adjourned when we finished. People were kind of immersing themselves in the calm and joy of Unity's presence. Then they went to their cars to go home. I'm not sure what reaction you will get tomorrow, but it was quite an experience."

"Thanks for calling and telling me, Barbara. I really appreciate all the leadership you are giving. How did you know that the parent association was meeting this evening?"

"Mr. Brewer called Randy's dad and suggested that Randy and his friends attend as they may be needed to explain some of their thinking and activities. So, Mr. Lubienski called each of us, and our parents brought us to the Timber Ridge School."

Chapter Twenty

The days and weeks passed, and to everyone's surprise and happiness, the project was seeming to work in each school. The unification was becoming a reality. People were appreciating people's efforts to make the transformation happen.

At the end of the pilot, the evaluation specialist was able to show academic and social gains of children. Attitudes were clearly changing. It would be erroneous to say that all was perfect, because it wasn't. It was positive enough to give people confidence in the belief that they were doing the right thing.

The decisions were made by the teachers and parents in each school to expand the pilots to include additional teachers and children. In addition to Randy, four Winterhaven students who had been attending the Timber Ridge School transferred their enrollment to Winterhaven, and their transition was working out quite well.

As predicted, the program became popular. The word was getting around that change was happening in Winterhaven. People from all over the state were wanting to visit. The children were asked to attend meetings in other school districts to explain what they had accomplished.

The State Superintendent of Schools called Superintendent Hosford and invited the students to give a presentation before the State Board of Education. Heather accepted before even asking the children and their parents, because she was convinced that this was the ticket to change in many other districts. She knew that the change had to come from a transformation of attitude, and she feared that people learning about the success in Winterhaven would think they could just go to their school district and implement the program. The change would have to come from the heart, and as in Winterhaven, from the children.

The committees to look into law and finance completed their work in a matter of months and they were able to provide a set of recommendations that led to the Winterhaven School District's capturing all the available dollars it was entitled to. To everyone's surprise, they were in compliance with applicable state and federal laws. They had accomplished what would seem to be impossible. They took a fiscal and legal system based on separation and turned it into a unifying force to benefit all.

Dr. Hosford was on her way to work and it was the middle of winter. She approached the city park where she had met Unity several months earlier. In the meantime, her school district had undergone a transformation many would have believed to have been impossible. She pulled into the park which had snow drifts as high as the car. She parked close to where she had met Unity and just closed her eyes in silence for a moment. When she opened her eyes she saw Unity standing beside the road. She motioned for her to join her in the warmth of her car.

"Well, Unity, it's working. The children did it. We're unifying the district and almost everyone feels comfortable with the change."

"Yes, the change came from the children."

"No, the change came from you, Unity. You were the one who appeared to them and gave them the ideas and the guidance for the change."

"All they did was recognize who they are. It is quite simple. They knew in their souls that all of life is unified. All the trouble in the world stems from the simple thought that we are separate. As soon as people awake to the truth that they are bound by love, all pain, suffering, hate, anger, and injustice will cease. It has to cease because it is inconsistent with our connectedness in love."

"The changes are happening in Winterhaven, but I don't know if anyone besides the children and a few of us that you touched are seeing the connectedness."

"Some need the truth told to them bluntly and others learn the truth by becoming it. The day-to-day activity of unity will lead to people becoming connected. Change occurs in both ways. Some come into it and others need to have a significant event to realize it. Both have happened and will continue to happen in Winterhaven."

"Will we be up to the task of helping all who want to learn from us?" Heather asked.

"Yes. The children will establish the SUPPORT Foundation."

"What is that?" Heather asked.

"I met with them a while ago. They were thinking about a way to continue their work and to provide support to other students who want to create positive change, in their school districts. Brad suggested a foundation where contributions could lead to a center where students would come for retreats much like their experience at the sanctuary."

"That is a great idea!" Heather exclaimed.

"They thought so. This way they'll be able to help many other children."

"Love just expands and expands, doesn't it," Heather said noticing that her side window was fogging a bit. She turned to wipe it clear. When she turned back to Unity, she was gone. Once again the peace and the calm were present. She waited a moment and gave thanks for Unity's presence and the love she gives to all.

When Dr. Hosford got to her office, Eleanor said that Mr. Brewer was on the phone and wanted to talk to her. "Hi, Phil. How're you?"

"I'm doing just fine. Got a minute?"

"Sure. What's on your mind?"

"My board wants to meet with your board sometime in the future."

"What might be the topic of discussion?" Heather asked. "I ask even though I have a pretty good idea of what you're going to say."

"No, I think you'll be surprised. They want to talk about unification from a different perspective."

"Please explain."

"Barbara, Emily, Brad, and Randy have met with the parents since Unity spoke with them. Instead of dismantling our school, they'd like to consider welcoming students to learn in our school and to use all of our unique facilities for the benefit of everyone."

"Interesting Phil. I guess once you feel connected, the place becomes irrelevant."

"I think so. They're thinking of many ways to reach out and welcome everyone to our school. They even want to change the name of the school. I think they want to start off with a fresh concept."

Unity and the Children

Mrs. O'Brien seemed to strike a chord with everyone when she said something like, 'When we are connected, and I believe this by the way, the place where one goes to school isn't important. What is important is the attitude of all the people. If the place promotes separation as Timber Ridge currently does, then perhaps it should change. But if this school, this collection of brick and mortar and all the people in it feel connected, then it fits the education complex just like Toboggan Run, Snow Castle, and Northern Lights. So, I believe we need to cease our separatist thinking. The children are right, but I repeat, we don't need to dismantle this school. Rather, I think we open our doors and our minds to discover ways to connect. We've wonderful resources, people, and ideas.'"

"That's wonderful, Phil."

"I thought you'd think so. One more thing, the students are going to ask the board to allow one of the our rooms to be used for the SUPPORT Foundation. I'm telling you so you won't be surprised."

"I've already heard about the Foundation idea."

"That's not possible. I heard Brad give the idea ten minutes ago in a meeting. I know he couldn't have talked with you since he said it."

"Maybe I just thought I heard about the Foundation idea" Heather said with a smile. "It doesn't matter. Let's just say when you are connected and joined in love that ideas can flow through the energy that connects us all."

"You won't get any disagreement from me. Have a good day, Dr. Hosford."

"Thanks for your call. Bye."

Chapter Twenty-One

The end of the year all school banquet was always held the first Saturday evening in June. Dr. Hosford traditionally gives a speech and several members of the staff are recognized for their accomplishments. The school board attends as does most of the staff and administrators. After dinner and introductions, Dr. Hosford addressed the group. "When our school year began, we decided to listen to four students who had a vision of unification. We trusted them and followed their message of connectedness. In all of my years in education, I've never seen the impact of a group of people as I've seen this year. Not only am I proud of Barbara, Emily, Brad, and Randy, but I'm proud of each of you. You all took a risk in listening to these children and in changing the way you teach and administer. Your willingness to work together helped all of us realize that we, too, are connected in our mission to provide a quality education for all of the students and I do mean all of the children of Winterhaven.

"At this time, I would like to have Barbara Conrad and her mother Valerie; Emily Hernandez and her mother Marie and her father Joe; Brad and his foster parents Mr. and Mrs. Sommers and his grandmother Marilyn Proudfoot; and Randy Lubienski and his father Bob and stepmother Linda come forward." There was a sustained round of applause as all twelve made their way to Dr. Hosford.

"Thank you for believing in us and our vision of unification," Barbara said when she arrived at the podium. "On behalf of Emily, Brad, and Randy I want to express our sincere appreciation to Dr. Hosford. She came to our leadership conference and listened to us, believed in us, and supported us. We also want to thank all of the Winterhaven students, parents, teachers, administrators as well as the parents, teachers, students and staff of the Timber Ridge School for their open hearts and minds. We especially thank Mr. Traylor who listened, guided, and was there for us.

"Emily, Brad, Randy, and I are working to establish a SUPPORT Foundation so that all the good that has happened in Winterhaven can happen in other districts because of children who see the connectedness, and who will not accept separation. Thank you, and especially we thank Unity, who is our loving guide and our source of strength. We love you, Unity, and we love all of you."

When Barbara finished, everyone in the banquet hall stood and gave the thirteen individuals a standing ovation. As they acknowledged the love coming toward them, they noticed Unity in the audience smiling and clapping in unison with all. They smiled back and knew that she was present in their heart, and soul, at this moment and forever.

The End

Unity and the Children

Then Yahweh answered and said, "Write the vision down, inscribe it on tablets to be easily read, since the vision is for its own time only; eager for its own fulfillment; it does not deceive; if it comes slowly, wait, for come it will, without fail."

Hab. 2:2-4

Discussion Questions for Teachers, Parents, and Facilitators

1. How can we develop a Unity consciousness in our school, community, family, or place of worship?

2. What activities can we carry out that would assist in feeling a sense of connectedness in our family, school, community, or place of worship?

3. What can we do as individuals, a class, or a group of people to inspire others to adopt an attitude of connectedness?

4. What might be some of the benefits of living a life whereby we envision a sense of connectedness?

5. How can we begin or continue to serve others, but to do so out of compassion which will come from a knowing that we are all one?

6. How can our unique personalities and our physical presence on this earth be celebrated once we accept that we are connected?

7. This book concentrated on a school system. Can you envision another setting where change could be beneficial when people learn that they are connected?

8. Have you ever had a Unity experience?

9. Unity was comfortable in nature. Do you sense life's energy and a connection in nature?

Note: Please let us know what questions surfaced or better yet, what answers were provided when people discussed *Unity and the Children*. Each comment will be read and studied with much interest.

The Children's Principles

1. Our differences are perceived by our senses. We are in fact connected and are part of one another.
2. Any system, procedure, words, or activity that reinforce separation must be dissolved.
3. If any procedure, process, or activity is good for one, it is good for all.
4. We celebrate our differences as they remind us that we must support each other at all times.

———⬥———

The Children's Belief Statement

Beyond what our physical senses perceive, which is a world of separateness, is our knowing that we are all connected by love. Knowing that we are connected leads to unconditional love which results in kindness and compassion and service.

Richard L. Baldwin

About the Author

Richard L. Baldwin has enjoyed a long career in special education. He has been a 6th grade teacher, a teacher of children with hearing impairments, has worked in teacher preparation programs at Kent State University and Texas Tech University. Rich spent 20 years as a consultant, supervisor, and director of the Office of Special Education Services in the Michigan Department of Education.

In 1997, Rich established a publishing company and has self-published a series of special education mysteries entitled, the Louis Searing and Maggie McMillan Mystery Series. He has also written a booklet entitled *The Piano Recital* and he honored his most favorite part of Michigan, the Upper Peninsula by writing *A Story to Tell—Special Education in the Upper Peninsula of Michigan:1902-1975*. Rich lives in Haslett, Michigan with his wife, Patty, and their two cats, Luba and Millie.

About the Artist

Joyce Gard, who paints under the name of J. Lily, received a B.A. degree in art in the late 60s. In 1991 she was awarded a scholarship from the Kalamazoo Institute of Art to study life drawing and won the 1998 Individual Artists Award from the Arts Council of Kalamazoo. In 1997 she was asked to read *Unity and the Children*. This book touched her soul and she agreed to paint a picture portraying Unity. She notes that Unity was often in nature before speaking with the characters in the book. Unity notes that "I love to be in nature. Being alone and silent are what I enjoy whenever I can." J. Lily's painting utilizes colors that resonate energy and unity. They depict the spirit of Unity as love. Unity is looking up to the reddish pink sky which to the artist represents the color of love. It is a quiet time in nature where Unity's spirit and God's spirit are connecting, energizing, and being filled with love prior to meeting with the children and connecting in love with them.

Joyce resides in Kalamazoo, Michigan, where she works for Western Michigan University as an Administrative Assistant in the Department of Speech Pathology and Audiology.

Richard L. Baldwin

Other Books by Richard L. Baldwin

The Piano Recital

A Story to Tell: The History of Special Education
in Michigan's Upper Peninsula

The Louis Searing and Margaret McMillan Mystery Series:

A Lesson Plan for Murder

The Principal Cause of Death

Administration Can Be Murder (Coming out in early 2000)

Buttonwood Press Order Form

Name _____

Address _____

City/State/Zip _____

Book Title	Quantity	Price
Unity and the Children ($12.95 – Hardcover)		
The Piano Recital ($6.95 – Softcover)		
A Story to Tell: The History of Special Education in Michigan's Upper Peninsula ($10.00 – Softcover)		
A Lesson Plan for Murder ($12.95 – Softcover)		
The Principal Cause of Death ($12.95 – Softcover)		
Administration Can Be Murder ($12.95 – Softcover) (Coming out in early 2000)		
Subtotal		
Michigan 6% Sales Tax		
Shipping & Handling ($1.50 per book)*		
TOTAL		

*If purchasing more than 5 books, please contact Buttonwood Press for bulk rates.

Mail Order Form with a Check payable to:

Buttonwood Press   Fax: 517-339-5908
PO Box 716   Email: RLBald@aol.com
Haslett, MI 48840   Website: www.buttonwoodpress.com

Contribution Policy

Buttonwood Press has a long-standing reputation of contributing $1.00 from each book sold to organizations serving persons with disabilities. One dollar from each copy of *Unity and the Children* sold will be forwarded to a Foundation. This Foundation, to be called The Unity Foundation, will award grants to schools or groups who wish to pursue the Principles and the Belief Statement of the Children. For more information, please visit the Buttonwood Press website at www.buttonwoodpress.com